FLAWSOME LIVES IN INDIA

Embracing the Chaos with Laugh and Wink

Pratyaya Jagannath

INDIA • SINGAPORE • MALAYSIA

Contents

Gratitude

Born and raised in the rustic charm of northern Odisha near Jharkhand, I discovered an insatiable love for stories early on. My "bookshelf" (a fancy word for a pile of books) was packed with translated classics like *Treasure Island*, *Robin Hood*, and *The Three Musketeers*, which whisked me away on adventures beyond my humble surroundings, aided by my vibrant friends Sabuja and Shivaji.

A curious observer and decent student, I soon packed my bags for Xavier Institute of Management, Bhubaneswar, where I earned an MBA in Rural Management. My professional journey began in northern India, where Delhi gave me its chaos, culture, and heat (enough to question my survival skills). Later, I found myself in the snowy embrace of Cornell University, pursuing a master's in international development while marvelling at global friendships, surprise blizzards, and portion sizes that could feed an Odia wedding.

This book is my attempt to turn observations into laughs. Inspired by the brilliant wit of Tattwa Prakash Satapathy (Papu Pom Pom), Varun Grover, and Late Shri Raju Srivastava, I have infused real-life hilarity into fiction. My family deserves credit for their humour and resilience—my parents, Minati Mishra and Jagannath Panda, my wife Shipra, my daughter Samhita, and my cheer squad: Deshna, Ashish, and small Kishu.

A special ode to my niece Aditi Sahu, whose boundless enthusiasm and constant cheer reignited my passion for writing and kept it burning brightly through doubts and distractions. Her encouragement reminded me of the power of dreams—no matter how long they have been on pause. Without Aditi, this book may have stayed a wistful thought instead of a tangible reality.

I am also grateful to my extended family, Dr Aditya Narayan Sahu, Dr Yoshaskam Agnihotri, Dr Jijnasu Agnihotri, Dr Namratha, Ms Madhusmita Sahu, and Dr Prapti, for reminding me that humour is a survival skill in a family of overachievers.

Here is to find the flawsome in every twist and turn of life—and laughing all the way through it!

Delivery Democracy: The Rise of the Tomatoes Knights and Swingy Spartans

In a *pioneering* (read: "What were they thinking?") decision passed at precisely **01:04 AM**, the government has declared that **delivery drivers** from **Swingy, Tomatoes, Romino's, and Pizza Pot** will now hold the same legal status as **ambulance drivers**. Yes, you heard that right. Move aside, traffic laws—there is a **new emergency service** in town, with extra cheese and a side of fries.

The Culinary Code Red: Make Way for the Food Warriors

From this moment on, seeing an orange Swingy T-shirt or a red Tomatoes bag zooming toward you is your cue to **scatter like pigeons in a park**. No sirens, no honks—just the silent, sacred urgency of your midnight biryani screaming for delivery. "A hungry customer is now classified as a **national crisis**," declared the **Ministry of Traffic Affairs and Midnight Munchies** in an oddly poetic press release. *"A delay in food delivery is akin to a constitutional emergency; one must act swiftly or face the consequences of an unholy, hangry uprising."*

Pedestrian crossings? Traffic lights? Speed limits? Forget them all. The delivery driver is now **above mortal restrictions**, zooming through traffic with the finesse of a Formula One (F1) racer who is late for his mom's lunch. If you dare to block their path, the punishment is swift: a **two-hour seminar, "How Not to Be a Hangry Monster,"** hosted by a government official who has not eaten in three days for "research."

The Hunger Games: Late Delivery Edition

The esteemed government has clarified that the **hunger status of delivery drivers is irrelevant**. *"They are not mere humans,"* the official decree reads, *"but warriors of the gig economy, transcending hunger, fatigue, and common sense."* It does not matter if the delivery boy has not eaten since yesterday or if it looks like he might keel over any second. What matters is the **customer's existential dread** over soggy fries or lukewarm pizza.

Customers, meanwhile, have been given full authority to unleash their fury. Was your burger 90 seconds late? Write a strongly worded complaint, compose a breakup letter to the app, or better yet, pen a **Shakespearean sonnet of suffering** and recite it from your balcony for dramatic effect. After all, if your pasta arrives cold, it is not just a dreadful day—it is a **culinary apocalypse**.

Weather? What Weather?

Regarding delivery, the weather is now officially classified as an **inconsequential inconvenience**. Rain? A drizzle of challenge. Thunderstorms? Background music. Cyclones? Just a refreshing breeze for our brave delivery warriors.

The new bill subtly suggests that **no force of nature—**not hurricanes, floods, or even an alien invasion—should interfere with the sacred mission of getting garlic bread to your doorstep. Suppose there is a literal Bollywood dance-off in the middle of the street. In that case, the delivery driver is expected to pirouette through it like a caffeinated ballet dancer. Because *"The show (and the delivery) must go on."*

Tipping Is for Quitters

The government has also abolished the concept of tipping. Why reward someone who braved traffic, wild dogs, and the wrath of monsoon winds to bring you food? Instead, you are encouraged to test their patience. Ask them to climb six floors because *"the lift isn't working,"* then demand to know why they did not bring extra ketchup packets. Want to express your gratitude? Compose a **haiku of blame** or leave a glowing review like, *"Delivery was fast, but the smile was 30% less enthusiastic than I expected."*

Extreme Priority Zones: The Fast and the Furious

The heart of the bill lies in the creation of **Extreme Priority Zones**. In this dystopian reality, delivery drivers have more freedom than your annoying cousin who "borrowed" your car and never returned it. These zones allow them to ignore all rules, including gravity, if needed. If you see a delivery guy speeding past a red light, weaving through pedestrians, and **dodging cows like they are**

playing Temple Run, know that they are doing God's (or your stomach's) work.

Pedestrians are advised to carry helmets and kneepads for safety. Vegetable vendors? Better get turbo wheels for your carts. And cyclists? Just stay home.

The New Emergency Siren: The T-Shirt Code

Ambulances have their sirens, but these culinary heroes have something even more iconic: **their T-shirts**. The sight of Swingy Orange or Tomatoes Red now demands instant respect. "It's like seeing a superhero cape," a Ministry of Gig Economy Heroes spokesperson explained. Citizens are encouraged to bow in reverence and whisper a silent prayer as these warriors zoom past, delivering paneer tikka to its destination.

The National Salute to Delivery Heroes

In conclusion, the government urges all citizens to embrace this **bold new reality** with open arms and empty stomachs. The next time you hear a screech of tyres and see a delivery boy balancing five orders on his scooter, step aside, salute, and remember: you are witnessing the dawn of a new era. In this era, **food delivery is a matter of national importance**.

And when your food finally arrives—hot, cheesy, and perfectly timed—do not forget to take a moment to appreciate the warrior who made it happen. Then complain about the missing cutlery because, hey, traditions matter too.

2

The Great Domestic Battlefield: A Husband's War Diary

Marriage, they said, is a **partnership of equals**. They did not tell me that it is also a **daily battlefield**, where the rules of engagement are written in disappearing ink, and the Geneva Convention is a distant rumour. My wife is a tactical genius—a **General Patton of cleanliness, logic, and memory**, armed with an arsenal of household laws that I, the hapless infantry soldier, can neither understand nor escape.

The Laundry List of My Defeats

1. **Arguments: A Fantasy for the Unmarried**

   Arguing with my wife is like entering a court where she is both the lawyer and the judge, and I am the defendant whose lawyer did not show up. She can counter any point with the precision of a Supreme Court senior advocate while I flounder like a kid who forgot his lines at a school debate.

   The last time I tried to justify leaving the bathroom light on, she attacked me with three-pronged attacks: rising energy bills, global warming statistics, and an ancient Sanskrit proverb about wastefulness. When she concluded her closing arguments, I was ready to apologise to humanity and the environment.

2. Cleanliness: Her Holy Doctrine

To her, **cleanliness is not just next to godliness—it is the religion itself.** If a crumb falls on the floor, she materialises out of thin air, armed with a broom and a glare that could crumble mountains. Once, I spilt Rajma on the couch, and I swear she looked at me like I had committed treason against the state.

"Do you realise," she said dramatically, "that you're building an entire **ecosystem under the dining table?**" Before I could blink, she had handed me a dustpan and assigned me a crash course in ecosystem destruction.

3. Her Civic Superpowers

My wife has the **civic awareness of a Swachh Bharat ambassador**, whereas I sometimes forget my own PIN code. She knows the **garbage truck schedule, water supply timings, and even the local MLA's hobbies.**

Once, during a lecture on civic responsibility, she asked me, "Do you even know who our ward councillor is?"

"Of course," I lied confidently. "It's... um... Sharma Ji?"

Her glare confirmed I had just failed yet another household civics test.

4. Dressing Like a Disaster

Wearing mismatched socks and an un-pressed shirt is not "quirky" but **"socially unacceptable."** Her idea of dressing involves colour coordination, polished shoes, and a checklist longer than my grocery list.

When I wore slippers to a wedding, she stared at me like I had shown up in a towel. "You look like a lost tourist in your city," she sighed before dragging me to the nearest store to buy proper footwear.

5. The Eternal Mistake

The worst battlefield of all? The **mistake I made five years ago.** I forgot what I had for breakfast yesterday, but she remembered this 4K Ultra HD incident. "Remember when you forgot our anniversary and said, 'Oh, was that today?'" she reminds me monthly, like a Netflix series that refuses to be cancelled.

The Ultimate Resistance: Food Boycott

Having lost every argument, every debate, and every shred of dignity, I have developed a **revolutionary resistance strategy: boycotting her favourite foods.**

She loves *rajma chawal* (kidney beans and rice) and *chhole chawal* (chickpeas and rice), which she cooks perfectly. My rebellion? Refusing to eat them. Every time she lovingly serves rajma chawal, I say with feigned heroism, "I'm not hungry."

Her glare says, *"Traitor!"* but my smirk says, *"Victory is mine—this time."*

My younger brother, who faces similar tyranny, has joined the movement. His weapon of defiance? **Boycotting golgappas** (crunchy puris filled with tangy water and potatoes). We are the **Che Guevaras of culinary rebellion**, united by our refusal to eat snacks that bring our wife's joy.

Her Counterattack: Emotional Blackmail

But my wife, ever the strategist, knows how to counter this resistance. She cooks rajma chawal, serves herself a generous portion, and sits next to me with an Oscar-worthy sigh:

"I guess you don't love me anymore."

Once, I caved and took a bite. Big mistake! She immediately exclaimed, "Aha! You could not resist! Admit it—I am right about everything!" She celebrated like she had just won the cricket World Cup while I sat there, defeated yet again, wishing rajma did not taste so good.

The Aftermath: Small Wins, Big Losses

For every crumb I clean, every mismatched sock I hide, and every rajma chawal I boycott, she finds new ways to assert her dominance. She is undefeated, and I am the **perpetually overrun infantry soldier**.

But I have small wins, like the **golgappa-free alliance** with my brother. We hold the line together, fighting for the dignity of men who forgot their anniversaries and wore slippers to weddings.

The War That Never Ends

And so, the battle continues. She fights with intelligence, wit, and an elephant's memory, while I resist with boycotted meals and poorly timed silences. Deep down, though, I know the truth: **this is a war I can never win.**

Because for every victory I claim, she will remind me of the socks I left on the dining table, the rajma I spilt, or the anniversary I forgot.

But hey, at least I have my brother. We will fight the good fight together—**one missed golgappa and skipped rajma chawal at a time—until** dinner, at least.

3

The Great Delhi Sewer Games: A Saga of Survival and skill

In the heart of Delhi, where chaos and resilience collide, lies a world like no other: the **urban villages**. These labyrinthine settlements are where history plays hopscotch with modernity, and both promptly tumble into an open sewer. It is a place where **innovation is born out of necessity**, and every corner tells a story of survival with a punchline sharp enough to cut through the stench.

The Olympic Trials Begin: Sewer Gymnastics Unveiled

It all started with **Ramesh Bhai**; the local legend whose viral video turned the world's attention to the athletic prowess of Delhi's urban villagers. The footage showed him vaulting over a 10-foot garbage mound with a finesse that could make Olympic gymnasts weep.

"It's not just jumping," explained Ramesh, adjusting his flip-flops. *"It's about survival."*

His feet had not touched dry ground in years, yet his balance remained impeccable.

Soon, gymnasts worldwide arrived to train in these natural obstacle courses. Babloo, another local hero, scoffed at their enthusiasm:

"Yeh log parkour bolte hain?" (They call this parkour?) *"Hum toh Mughalon ke zamane se gutter ke upar kood rahe hain."* (We have been jumping over sewers since the Mughal era.)

Babloo introduced the newcomers to his signature move: the **"Triple Flip Sewer Avoidance Maneuver"**—a combination of acrobatics and sheer instinct perfected over years of dodging questionable puddles.

The Chess Masters Enter the Game

Not to be outdone, **chess grandmasters** arrived to test their skills navigating the village's treacherous maze. Sergey Karjakin, a former world champion, described the experience as *"like a chessboard, but with open drains instead of squares."*

Standing on a precariously dry patch of ground, Sergey calculated his next move:

"Knight to D4—or should I say, Step to Dry Floor?"

Locals quickly turned this into a spectator sport, placing bets on which grandmaster would misstep into a sludge-filled pothole first.

"Kasparov beat Deep Blue," chuckled Munna, a local bookie, *"but let's see him dodge that manhole."*

The Urban Village Starter Pack

While the world marvelled at their resilience, the locals carried on with their lives, fuelled by a **starter pack** that included:

1. **Hukkah Lounges**

   Every lane boasts a hukkah lounge where locals gather to discuss topics ranging from gym routines to global politics, all while exhaling clouds of mint-flavoured smoke.

   - *"Sure, the sewer stinks,"* said Rajesh, flexing his biceps, *"but we stink of ambition."*

2. **Luxury Cars and Drains**

   Fortuners and BMWs jostle for space in lanes barely wide enough for a cycle.

   - *"Gaadi toh honi chahiye, chahe sewer ke upar kyun na ho,"* (A car is essential, even if it is parked over a sewer) said Sunil, a landowner who rents out rooms to forty bachelors.

3. **Gym Bros**

   Local gyms are temples of muscle worship, where bodybuilders pump iron between sips of hukkah. Protein shakes are replaced with concoctions of eggs, bananas, and mysterious powders.

   - *"Hume toh Old Monk bhi protein lagta hai,"* (Even Old Monk feels like protein to us) joked one gym enthusiast.

Surviving the Streets: An Art Form

Walking through Delhi's urban villages is a **test of skill and nerve**. Locals have developed techniques that are part science, part choreography.

Sheila Aunty, a seasoned resident, proudly demonstrated her **"Zigzag Dry-Step"** technique.

"I haven't stepped in sludge in five years," she declared, showing off her spotless sandals.

Tourists, meanwhile, pay for **"Sewer Safari Tours,"** complete with a crash course in jumping over garbage, dodging rogue cows, and holding their breath near open drains.

- *"It's like Disneyland,"* said Pappu, the tour operator, *"but with more hazards."*

A Government Dilemma: Fix or monetise?

The government's sudden international fame left it in a dilemma. Should it fix the open drains or turn the villages into **UNESCO World Heritage Sites**?

- *"Why spend money on repairs when we can charge tourists?"* asked a local councillor, sipping tea next to a pile of garbage.

Bureaucrats even floated the idea of branding the villages as **"Sewer Start-Up Hubs,"** claiming the resilience of their residents embodied the true spirit of **Make in India**.

A Culinary Adventure: Fearless Eating

No story of Delhi's urban villages is complete without mentioning the **culinary courage** of its residents.

- **Chhole Bhature Stalls** boasts oil that has been reused more than Bollywood storylines. *"Yeh oil toh hamare dadaji ka hai,"* (This oil is from my grandfather's time) said one vendor proudly.

- **Golgappa Stalls** double as immunity clinics. *"Yeh paani nahi, ek vaccine hai,"* (This is not water, it is a vaccine) joked a regular customer, popping another golgappa like it was a vitamin pill.

Where There's Muck, There's Magic

Despite the chaos, Delhi's urban villages are a testament to **human ingenuity and humour**. Residents have turned their daily struggles into a spectacle, welcoming gymnasts, chess grandmasters, and adventurous tourists alike.

As Babloo says:

"Yahan sewer nahi, ek lifestyle hai." (It is not just a sewer; it is a lifestyle.)

Because in the **Great Delhi Sewer Games**, there are no losers—just survivors with stories to tell and shoes that desperately need a wash.

The Great Indian Barber Shop Chronicles: Where Scissors Meet Saviour

Stepping into an Indian barbershop is not just about getting a haircut—it is about stepping into a microcosm of **chaos, wisdom, and sheer unpredictability**, where the air smells of talcum powder, hair oil, and existential dread. Every visit is a **mini soap opera** where you walk in as a mortal but leave feeling like you have survived an unsanctioned experiment.

The Name Game: Barber Branding Brilliance

Indian barbershops have a knack for choosing names that range from bizarre to outright plagiaristic. A simple walk down any street will reveal gems like:

- **Google Doodle Hair Lounge** (SEO-friendly if nothing else).

- **Salmaan Hair Craft** (not Salman Khan, but close enough).

- **Cut & Glow Studio** (because "glow" after a haircut is a priority).

Inside, Bollywood posters share space with religious idols, LED lights flicker like a disco, and in the corner, there is always that one bottle of **"Cool King Hair Oil"** perched like it is the **crown jewel of grooming**.

The Great Cool Oil Massacre

No Indian barber experience is complete without the **fabulous oil scalp massage**.

The Sales Pitch:

"Bhaiya, ek baar lagwa lo. Stress free, thanda mast lagega!" (Try it once, it is cool and stress-free!)

The Reality:

A palmful of oil is dumped onto your scalp before the barber kneads **your head like dough**. He chops, slaps, and pounds until you question your life choices. By the end, you are less a customer and more a **shiny beacon for maritime navigation.**

The Aftermath:

Your hair gleams like it have been dunked in a vat of frying oil, and your neck feels like it has endured a **WWE smackdown**.

The Playlist: Songs for Every Snip

The barbershop playlist is a **musical time machine:**

1. **The Nostalgic Barber:** Kumar Sanu and Alka Yagnik crooning melodramatic nineties ballads.

2. **The Trendy Apprentice**: Punjabi rap that no one understands, but everyone bobs too.

3. **The Default Anthem**: Salman Khan's *Oh Oh Jaane Jaana* plays on repeat because, let us face it, **Bhai is God here.**

Sometimes, the barber hums along, adding his own off-key twist because what is a haircut without some live karaoke?

The Philosophical Gossip Session

Barbers are not just hairdressers—they are **neighbourhood philosophers**, dispensing unsolicited advice with every snip.

Politics:

"Petrol price Elon Musk ke SpaceX ke vajah se badh raha hai." (Petrol prices are rising because of SpaceX!)

Cricket:

"Virat Kohli ko calm hona chahiye. Dhoni jaisa patience kahan milega!" (Virat Kohli needs to calm down; no one can match Dhoni's patience!)

Your Life Choices:

"Beard kaafi achi hai, lekin agar facial karwaoge toh ladki impress ho jayegi." (Your beard is excellent, but a facial will impress the ladies.)

By the end, you are questioning if you came for a haircut or a **TED Talk in Hindi**.

The Tools of Torture

Hygiene at these shops is more of a **suggestion than a standard**:

- **Combs** that have brushed more scalps than an election campaign.

- **Razors** sharpened on a mysterious stone that looked like it had been excavated from a Harappan site.

- **Towels** that double as relics, soaked in decades of sweat, talc, and forgotten dreams.

Bleach, Facials, and Financial Ambush

You walk in for a ₹100 haircut, but by the end, the barber has convinced you to try a **bleach-facial combo** for ₹1,000.

The Pitch:

"Sir, aapka face glow karega. Ladkiyan fida ho jayengi!" (Sir, your face will glow, and women will adore you!)

The Result:

Your face burns with the intensity of a thousand suns, and you leave looking like a cross between **a K-pop idol and a cautionary tale.**

The Bone-Breaking Massage

Every barber believes in ending the session with a **complimentary assault on your nervous system.**

The scalp massage morphs into a full-blown **neck-cracking session** that makes you wonder if they are moonlighting as chiropractors. And just when you think it is over, they whip out the **vibrating massage machine**, which does not so much soothe as it shakes your soul.

The Apprentice Chronicles

Every shop has the **ustaad (expert barber)** and his fumbling apprentice. Watching the latter is both hilarious and terrifying.

"Yeh kya kiya? Foam idhar lagao! Beard ka shape mat bigaado!" (What are you doing? Apply the foam here! Do not mess up the beard shape!)

Meanwhile, you sit frozen, praying the apprentice does not accidentally turn your haircut into a **performance art piece**.

The Upper Lip Shaving Saga

For those brave enough to get a shave, the **upper lip shave** is where courage meets calamity. The razor drags across your skin like a reluctant artist, and the finishing splash of alum feels like **liquid betrayal.**

The Barber Shop Olympics: Gossip and Games

With the rise of mobile gaming, barbershops now double as **esports arenas.**

"Free Fire khela? PUBG se better hai!"

(Played Free Fire? It is better than PUBG!)

Between haircuts, barbers and customers debate cheat codes, game strategies, and whether **GTA** is a metaphor for life.

A Symphony of Chaos and Cool Oil

An Indian barbershop is not just a place for grooming; it is a **stage for drama, humour, and existential revelations**. You walk in expecting a haircut and leave with a slightly crooked hairline, an oil-soaked scalp, and a story worth retelling.

Because at the end of the day, it is not just about looking good—it is about surviving the **Great Indian Barber Shop Chronicles** with your sanity and dignity (mostly) intact.

5

India Declares Haryanvi as the National Language: Flexing Tongues and Attitudes for Global Glory

India, the land of **19,500 languages (or more)**, has taken a bold leap into linguistic machoism by declaring **Haryanvi** the **national language**. Why? Diplomacy was not getting us anywhere, and the world needed a language that sounded like it could arm-wrestle Genghis Khan.

"When we say, 'Ke kar riya se?' (What are you doing?), it is not an interrogation—a warm greeting," clarified the **Minister of Cultural Cohesion**, a newly created role to manage the nationwide chaos caused by this decision.

Haryanvi: The Language of Muscle, Machoism, and Mockery

Proponents of Haryanvi argue that it is not just a language— it is a **state of mind**.

1. **Straight Talk, No Sugar-Coating**

   When a confused traveller at a Haryana railway station asks, *"When is the train coming?"* the answer is not a polite *"In 10 minutes."* Instead, it is:

"*Rail tale katke marega?*" (Will you die under the train?)

Brutally practical yet somehow compelling.

2. Directions with Personality

Lost tourists are also treated to Haryanvi-style directions:

"*Jahan se thandi hawa aavegi, udhar jaana.*" (Go where you feel the cold breeze.)

Translation: The canal is that way.

3. Insults That Hit Like a Tractor

The Haryanvi flair for mockery is unmatched. Call someone a fool, and they will counter with:

"*Baawli bhoot!*" (You foolish ghost!)

It is not just an insult but a character assassination with supernatural overtones.

The Case for Haryanvi: Why the World Needs It

1. Tone That Commands Respect

Haryanvi is **raw, direct, and consequential—**perfect for a country aiming to become a global powerhouse. "*Even our smallest sentence sounds like it's been bench-pressing at the gym,*" said a government official.

Imagine international diplomats quaking in their boots as India's representative thunders:

"Boll, kaun banega Vishwaguru?" (Tell us, who will be the world leader?)

2. **Efficiency Over Elegance**

   No room for fluffy language here. If you are wrong, you will know it in one syllable. *"Tu baitha reh, samajh aavegi"* (You will sit and understand) is both advice and a command.

3. **Global Diplomacy with a Local Twist**

   Imagine Haryanvi interpreters at the UN, delivering speeches that feel like an arm-wrestling match in words. World leaders will comply or pack up faster than a street vendor during a police raid.

Resistance from Across India: Everyone Wants a Word In Kannadigas: Kannada or Bust

In Karnataka, the battle cry was clear: *"Namma Kannada!"* (Our Kannada!). Auto drivers have become language tutors, greeting passengers with *"Kannada baruthe?"* (Do you know Kannada?) before offering impromptu lessons in grammar and survival phrases like ordering masala dosa.

One auto driver shared his patriotic mission: *"By the time I drop you, you'll know enough Kannada to complain about traffic."*

Marathis: Chhatrapati's Legacy vs. Akhadas

The **Marathis** were the first to object, with their iconic flair for drama. "Haryanvi as the national language?

What about **Marathi**, the language of **Chhatrapati Shivaji Maharaj**?" thundered a spokesperson at a rally in Pune.

"We've given India **Lavani, Powada**, and **vada pav**, and this is how you repay us?" he added, pausing to adjust his perfectly groomed moustache.

Protesters were heard chanting, *"Aamhi Punekar aahot!"* (We are Punekars!) while blocking traffic on Shaniwar Wada. A local bystander muttered, *"Wada pav chi queue sodun kaay milnar?"* (What will you gain by leaving the vada pav queue?)

Bengalis: Rabindra Sangeet and Intellectual Swag

Over in West Bengal, the **Bengalis** decided to take a more poetic approach. "If you want a national language, it should be **Bengali**—the language of **Tagore, Roy, and rosogollas**!" declared a protester on College Street, waving a book of Rabindranath Tagore's poems like a weapon.

Their slogans were as melodic as Rabindra Sangeet:

"Rosogolla amader, Bangla o amader!" (Rasgulla is ours and so is Bengali!)

One protestor explained, *"We already gave you the national anthem. Why not go all the way?"* Meanwhile, an intense argument broke out over the spelling of *"rosogolla"*, with one side insisting it is *"rasgulla"* and the other accusing them of cultural treason.

Tamil Nadu: Pure Tamil, Please!

Not to be outdone, Tamil Nadu issued its own ultimatum. "If Karnataka is making everyone learn Kannada, Tamil Nadu will stick to **only Tamizh**," declared a fiery minister.

"En vazhi, thani vazhi!" (My way is the only way!) he roared, quoting a famous Tamil film dialogue to emphasise the state's linguistic pride.

Protesters demanded the removal of English from all road signs, leaving tourists at the mercy of **Google Translate** or divine intervention. *"Who needs tourists when we have temples?"* reasoned one participant.

Northeast Voices: Khasi and Nagamese Demand Recognition

The **Northeast**, often sidelined in national discussions, made its voice heard.

- Khasi protesters marched with banners: *"Noh Hindi noh Haryanvi!"* (No Hindi, no Haryanvi!).

- In Nagaland, demonstrators chanted: *"Nagamese ase apuni bhasha!"* (Nagamese is our language!).

One activist said, *"We have been accommodating. Now it is time for India to teach others."*

Ravi Ashwin's Haryanvi Encounter: A Cricketing Sledge-Fest

After cricketer Ravi Ashwin's infamous Haryanvi sledging story, the announcement gained extra steam. While playing in Haryana, Ashwin faced bowlers who were as sharp with their words as they were with the ball.

One bowler shouted:

"Tu out nahi hoga? Yahan toh maidan ki mitti bhi mardangi ke saath girti hai!" (Won't you get out? Even the soil here falls with masculinity!)

Ashwin laughed off the incident but admitted, *"Playing in Haryana is as much a test of your batting as it is of your mental fortitude."*

The Forgotten Compromise: Sanskrit Revival

As the Haryanvi debate raged, some intellectuals proposed **Sanskrit** as a unifying choice. But historians pointed out that Sanskrit was historically the preserve of priests and scholars—not commoners. Critics joked: *"Sanskrit Seekho, Varna Chup Raho"* (Learn Sanskrit or stay quiet).

The Road Ahead: Linguistic Chaos and Global Glory

The government has promised a **23-part referendum**, with results expected by **2047**, perfectly timed for India's centenary. In the meantime, every region will keep fighting for its linguistic pride.

Haryanvi may not have everyone's approval, but its tone, swagger, and unique ability to answer a polite question with *"Rail tale katke marega?"* make it a strong contender for uniting—and intimidating—the world.

Because in India, where diversity is our strength, **chaos is our language**, and Haryanvi? That is just our way of flexing.

6

What Bihar Thinks Today, the World Thinks 200 Years Later

Picture this: I managed an entourage of lively agronomists from Latin America, all eager to unravel the secrets of Indian rice cultivation. Sounds straightforward, right? Wrong. Out of the entire group, **only one spoke English**, and my Spanish proficiency hovered somewhere between *"Hola"* and *"Gracias."* Suddenly, I was a translator, tour guide, and accidental comedian, juggling languages, fielding absurd questions, and desperately trying to look like I had everything under control.

Enter Bihar: The Land of Infinite Surprises

Our first stop was the legendary **Bodh Gaya, Bihar**, the birthplace of enlightenment and my initiation into a world where chaos and charm coexist. Through some serious networking (read: frantic WhatsApp messages to anyone remotely connected to Bihar), I secured the ultimate Bihar ride: a **Mahindra Scorpio.** Nothing says *"Bihar Experience"* like cruising rural roads in a vehicle that looks like it is auditioning for a role in *Fast & Furious: Village Drift.*

The Scorpio Chronicles: Bahubali on Wheels

The journey from Patna Airport to Bodh Gaya was less of a road trip and more of a **real-life video game**, complete with high-speed overtakes, sudden stops, and the occasional heart-stopping near-miss. Our Scorpio, a true **Bahubali (strongman)on wheels**, carved through narrow lanes like it was born to defy physics. Cows lounged nonchalantly in the middle of the road, trucks bore slogans like *"Horn OK Please"* that were more decorative than functional, and cycles carrying entire families (and sometimes goats) added to the adrenaline rush.

Despite the scenic chaos outside, the **rollercoaster effect** inside the Scorpio began taking its toll. My Latin American colleagues, who had arrived with wide-eyed excitement, were now holding onto the seats like their lives depended on it. Eventually, my boss—his patience as battered as the Scorpio's suspension—snapped: *"Get us a train back to Patna!"*

Bihar Trains: A Masterclass in Human Engineering

Booking train tickets in Bihar? A feat that makes climbing Everest seem like a leisurely hike. After hours of pleading, bribing, and begging at the ticket counter, I managed to secure seats—or so I thought. What awaited us was a **masterpiece of human engineering**, where "two humans under one seat" is not just a figure of speech but a **state of existence.**

The real treat came when someone casually strung a **hammock between two seats**, turning the train compartment into a makeshift campground. Chickens clucked from the luggage rack, bidis (local cigarettes) scented the air with their smoky charm, and gutkha (chewable tobacco) made its presence known with bright red splatters on the floor.

Peanut Shells and Philosophies

As our Latin American guests clutched their bags and patience, the passengers around us decided it was time for a conversation. Our standing presence and random bursts of *"Español"* piqued their curiosity. One uncle, proudly munching peanuts, struck up a chat. Topics ranged from *"Trumpwa"* (Donald Trump, now officially Bihari) to *"Obama kuch nahi karta"* (Obama does not do anything), with pit stops at demonetization, the rupee's struggles, and oil diplomacy.

A middle-aged gentleman, ever the gracious host, offered **my guests khaini (local chewable tobacco)**. Confused but polite, they declined, unsure whether it was food, medicine, or something requiring an antidote. Meanwhile, a lively debate on **fixing the Indian economy** unfolded, featuring more passion than a political rally and more solutions than any budget session.

Grit, Grace, and Gor Tho Kucha Raha Hai

When I thought I had seen it all, a passenger accidentally stepped on an elderly woman sitting on the floor. Her cry of *"Gor tho kucha raha hai!"* (Translation: "My leg hurts!") was a stark reminder that on a Bihar train, life is raw, honest, and remarkably unfiltered. Nobody paused to pity or placate; the train and the people moved on.

The Final Verdict

By the end of our trip, my Latin American friends had received a **crash course in Bihar's charm**—its rugged roads, colourful trains, and unapologetically raw spirit. They learned that **rice cultivation** was just one part of the lesson. The real takeaway? Bihar is not just a place; it is an experience, an adventure, and sometimes a survival test.

The journey was a humbling reminder of Bihar's **unique ability to marry chaos with wisdom**. While my agronomists flew home with tales of Scorpios, trains, and khaini, I left with a newfound respect for the **land where intellect meets improvisation**.

Because in Bihar, *what they think today, the world might think two hundred years later...*

The Great Red Revolution: Paan, Gutkha, and the Chronicles of Chewed-Up Chaos

Long ago, in the serene landscapes of ancient India, the Buddha—wise, tranquil, and undoubtedly free from dental plaque—advised his disciples to embrace silence. *"Speak less, listen more,"* he said, adding that silence was a mark of wisdom. Little did he know that this sage advice would one day be internalised not through meditation but through the curious combination of **Paan** and **Gutkha**—the silent yet vividly spitting duo that has painted modern India in fifty shades of red.

From Pure Breath to Paan Breath

Buddha's teachings emphasised pure breath—a focused, rhythmic inhalation to calm the mind. But pure breath alone seemed a bit bland for ancient Indians, who believed in adding spice to everything, even their enlightenment. Enter the **betel leaf**: an innocent green wrapper stuffed with areca nut, lime, cardamom, tobacco, and an entire spice rack's ingredient. This little packet did not just silence its chewers; it turned them into walking spittoons of red creativity.

The Odia, Bengalis, and people from Bihar embraced Paan as a culinary delight and a cultural statement. Chewing Paan was not just a habit—it was a lifestyle, a silent nod to Buddha's wisdom. After all, you cannot blurt out your foolishness when your mouth is stuffed with enough Paan to irrigate a small farm.

Kanpur: The Elon Musk of Gutkha

While the ancient betel leaf flourished across the subcontinent, modern times demanded convenience. Fresh leaves were not always accessible, and the hustle and bustle of cities called for a more portable option. This is when **Kanpur**—the Silicon Valley of Gutkha—stepped in. Kanpur did not just create Gutkha; it revolutionised it. A compact, leaf-free version of Paan, Gutkha became the **fast food of oral indulgence**, ready to be chewed and spat out anytime, anywhere.

Today, Kanpur's Gutkha industry unites Indians in silent camaraderie. From Assam to Gujarat, Gutkha enthusiasts can be identified by their trademark bulging cheeks, dreamy look of contentment, and impeccable aim when spitting. Gutkha's influence has transformed public walls, streets, and even monuments into crimson art galleries.

Spit Happens: The Art of Public Decoration

Let us talk about the **creative output** of Paan and Gutkha aficionados. This spontaneous splatter art adorns India's walls, sidewalks, and stairwells. Each red stain tells a story, whether a hurried spit during a traffic jam or a more calculated masterpiece on the pristine walls of a government office.

Taxi drivers have mastered the art of Gutkha disposal. Their technique involves cracking the car door just enough to lean out, releasing a precise arc of red, and closing the door with the flourish of an artist finishing a masterpiece. *"The road? It can handle it,"* one driver explained with a shrug, *"but the car seats? Too much effort to clean."*

Even historical monuments are not spared. Delhi's Red Fort (Lal Qila) is rumoured to owe its iconic hue to centuries of enthusiastic Paan chewers. Forget Mughal architecture—this is the legacy of saliva-fuelled patriotism.

From University Halls to Urban Legends

The influence of Paan and Gutkha starts early. University students like **Ravenshaw** and **Presidency College** hone their spitting skills on campus walls, turning blank spaces into abstract art installations. This talent matures over time, with alumni carrying their craft into corporate offices, train stations, and even the Madras High Court.

In some corners, the splatter has taken on mythical proportions. Locals whisper tales of the **"Phantom Spitter,"** a mysterious figure who leaves perfectly symmetrical red blotches on walls across Kolkata's metro stations. Is it an individual? A secret society? No one knows—but the artistry is undeniable.

The New Red Revolution: Paint the Town Red (Literally)

Paan and Gutkha's crimson stains have inspired more than just creative expression. They have rekindled the hopes of India's **Left Bloc**, whose political dominance has waned in recent decades. For Leftists, the red stains are a powerful symbol of revolution—proof that the colour red still reigns supreme in India, even if Marx and Lenin no longer do.

The movement has even crossed borders. Myanmar's junta has admired India's "Red Revolution," calling it a more profound cultural phenomenon than any military campaign. Papua New Guinea is rumoured to be considering Gutkha imports, inspired by the sheer audacity of India's red-tinted legacy.

Economics of Spit: From Dentists to Diplomacy

Not everyone is thrilled with the crimson chaos. Health organizations like the **WHO** regularly warn about Paan and Gutkha's links to oral cancer. But their warnings are drowned out by the booming economy these substances fuel. Dentists, oral surgeons, and ENT specialists are thriving, their clinics packed with red-stained mouths.

Meanwhile, the spice industry benefits from a peculiar side effect: dulled taste buds. Gutkha users demand blander food, creating a new market for *"tongue-tingling but mild"* dishes. Even regional delicacies are cashing in, with some earning Geographic Indication (GI) tags for their Gutkha-friendly flavours.

Cultural Chaos: The Vegetarian Connection

In a surprising twist, vegetarian societies have endorsed Paan and Gutkha as plant-based alternatives to meat-based indulgences. Their spokesperson, Mr. Bakra, recently declared, *"Chewing betel is the way to go—save animals, stain walls!"* Naysayers, however, recall the same organization's infamous claim that air pollution was caused by *"too many clouds."*

The Silent Legacy

Through all the chaos, one thing remains clear: Paan and Gutkha have given India a unique identity. From **taxi drivers perfecting their aim** to university students leaving their crimson mark on history, the legacy of these substances is woven into the nation's fabric—sometimes literally, as seen on countless shirts ruined by stray spits.

So next time you encounter a red-stained wall or dodge a flying arc of Gutkha, take a moment to appreciate the silent revolution behind it. This is not just a mess—it is a movement. Buddha wanted us to speak less and think more, and in their own bizarre way, Paan and Gutkha chewers have precisely achieved that.

Because in India, silence is not golden—it is **red, spicy, and occasionally splattered on the nearest wall**.

8

Mini Blood Banks of Odisha: A Mosquito Memoir

Odisha—the land of **pakhala** (fermented rice with water)-**fuelled naps**, Rasagola feuds, and an enduring ability to "Odia-fy" anything in sight. But beyond the sour-sweet charm of our culture exists a buzzing underworld, an organised syndicate more ruthless than any local politician and more persistent than a vendor selling *jhal muri* (spicy mixture of puffed rice). People welcome to the **mosquito menace** of Odisha—a satire-laden saga of tiny tyrants ruling a state of unsuspecting hosts.

Cuisine: A Mosquito's Pre-Feast Carnival

Odisha's culinary brilliance is a feast not just for humans but also for mosquitoes. Where else can you find idli and dosa paired unapologetically with **ghugni** (peas curry). This spiced green pea curry screams, *"Why stop at Sambhar when chaos tastes better?"*

Take the sacred **Dahi Vada** of Cuttack, a soft, tangy marvel loved by Odias everywhere—until Bhubaneswar got it firsthand. The humble vada has become a "breakfast bowl" of **cornflakes and seu (crispy gram flour snacks)**.

The Buzzing Bureaucracy: MASS in Action

Somewhere, a mosquito committee (**Mosquito Association of Sanguine Siphoners or MASS**) is nodding approvingly at this carb-loaded innovation, knowing it will deliver plump, sweetened bloodstreams for their midnight raids. Make no mistake—the **MASS** is the most well-organised entity in Odisha. While humans spar over urban drainage projects, MASS has quietly consolidated power, claiming every corner of the state as its own. Their strategy is impeccable.

First, they let the Odias settle into their **post-pakhala siestas**, when bodies are sprawled lazily on charpoys, leaving deliciously exposed limbs. But MASS is not about petty daytime nibbling. Oh no—they strike when the clock hits midnight, swarming in **synchronised battalions**. The sound of their collective buzz rivals the grandest performances of the **Konark Dance Festival**, albeit less pleasing to the ear.

By dawn, mosquito nets resemble a **Jackson Pollock painting** of blood splatters. At the same time, the bitten humans scratch furiously, adding percussion to this nocturnal opera.

Blood Banks Redefined: A Micro-Delivery Revolution

With Odisha often battling blood shortages, MASS has become the state's unofficial Red Cross partner. Why bother transporting blood in fancy refrigerated vans when

mosquitoes offer an ultra-micro delivery system? Imagine the ads:

"MASS: Delivering blood to the underserved, one itchy drop at a time. Bonus: free insomnia!"

Rural Odisha may have cow dung cakes for mosquito repulsion. Still, urban drains clogged with years of neglect are like luxury condominiums for the buzzing elites. While city dwellers frantically scratch their way through sleepless nights, MASS keeps the blood flowing—literally.

The Malaria Monopoly: A Retired Villain

Once upon a time, **Malaria** was Odisha's greatest villain, inspiring government campaigns, awareness drives, and frantic searches for the nearest mosquito net. But MASS has rendered malaria irrelevant. Why bother with a single disease when you can deliver an **itchy buffet of ailments**? Dengue, chikungunya, Zika—they have diversified their portfolio. Malaria is now a retired relic of simpler times, fondly remembered by nostalgic elders as *"woh purane dino ka bukhar" (that old day's fever)/*

Urban vs. Rural: A Tale of Two Itchy Worlds

In rural Odisha, the age-old cow dung cake—burnt like incense to ward off mosquitoes—has kept MASS at bay for generations. Urban Odisha, conversely, is a **mosquito paradise**, with its stagnant drains, uncovered garbage piles, and rooftop water tanks that double as mosquito swimming pools.

City folks scratch and sigh, wondering why they ever gave up the **fragrant cow-dung smoke of their village homes** while mosquitoes smugly feast on their sanitised, "modern" blood. Progress? Only for MASS.

A Tribute to the Buzzlords

Mosquitoes reign supreme in the land where sambhar becomes ghugni, and Dahi Vada gets a crunchy breakfast makeover. They are the true rulers of Odisha—a buzzing bureaucracy with no rivals, no elections, and absolutely no chill.

So, here is to Odisha, where the food is flavourful, the naps are sweet, and the mosquitoes genuinely live the high life. We scratch, swat, and sometimes curse, but we know this is true: the tiniest tyrants have turned our land of sour rice and sweet treats into their **mini blood bank.**

May your next mosquito bite come with a side of laughter—and a LOT of Odia resilience!

9

The Spiritual Spectrum: A Satsang of Stereotypes and Shenanigans

Welcome to India, where spirituality is not just a journey but a full-blown industry, complete with **branding, market segmentation, and promotional campaigns**. In this grand **bazaar of beliefs**, gurus are the CEOs, faith is the currency, and the **satsang** (holy mass) hall is a melting pot of hilarity, devotion, and precise product placement.

Let us explore this multi-tiered ecosystem, where enlightenment meets entertainment, and moksha comes with a subscription plan.

Group 1: The Rational Rebels (a.k.a. Freebie Philosophers)

This group consists of **intellectuals who attend satsangs like others binge TED Talks**—for the vibe, not the transformation. They sip overpriced green tea, drop words like *"mindfulness"* and *"existentialism,"* and nod sagely at phrases like, *"You are not your body; you are the observer of the observed."*

But when the donation box comes around? Their wallets are as closed as their minds are open. *"Spirituality is about detachment,"* they whisper as they quietly detach from contributing.

They ask questions designed to stump even the most seasoned guru:

- *"If karma is real, why are there so many potholes?"*
- *"If everything is an illusion, why is chai not free?"*

The guru, clearly exhausted, wishes he could chant the *"mute mantra"* and move on.

Group 2: The Half-Faithful and Half-Paying Pragmatists

This group straddles the line between scepticism and surrender. They want **peace of mind**, but they would also like a discount. Think of them as the **EMI enthusiasts of enlightenment**, armed with scripture quotes they found on Pinterest.

Their questions are as practical as they are perplexing:

- *"Is there a mantra to manifest a better credit score?"*
- *"Can mindfulness reduce my cholesterol?"*

They will donate, but only if the satsang hall has **air conditioning, free Wi-Fi, and tea that does not taste like boiled cardboard**. When the guru suggests giving more, they shrug and say, *"But you teach detachment, right? We are detached from overspending."*

Group 3: The Brand Loyalists of Bliss

Ah, the **middle-class spiritualists**. Their satsangs feel like a mix of multi-level marketing (MLM) pitch meetings and family picnics. For them, faith is semi-transactional, served with prasad in biodegradable packaging.

They adore their gurus, but not too deeply—they draw the line at waking up for 4 a.m. meditation. Their wallets are moderately open, but only for premium products:

- Guru-approved herbal teas? **Yes, please.**

- "Blessed" candles that smell like sandalwood and self-love? **Sold.**

- A subscription to the ashram's YouTube channel? **Only if it is ad-free.**

Their satsang highlight? **Selfies with the baba.** They caption them with "#Blessed #SpiritualJourney," carefully angling their donation receipt out of the frame to avoid awkward conversations about generosity.

Group 4: The Grassroots Devotees

This group embodies **pure, unadulterated devotion**, which Netflix could not script without trying. They do not care about buzzwords like *"cosmic alignment"* or *"quantum chakras."* Their faith is practical, personal, and often lifesaving.

For them, satsangs are not just spiritual gatherings but also **community events**, complete with langars (community meals), match-making opportunities, and, occasionally, **free medical camps**.

When asked to donate, they do not hesitate, even if it means dipping into their **hard-earned savings**. Without asking why the baba needs a platinum-plated meditation cave, they will fund the gufa-building project (cave fund).

The Gurus: Spiritual CEOs of the Modern Age

Every guru knows their audience like a **Netflix algorithm on steroids**, tailoring their teachings to maximise donations and devotion:

1. **For Group 1 (The Freebie Philosophers):**

   They whip out phrases like, *"You're not just stardust; you're the whole galaxy,"* and toss in a bit of quantum physics. The result? They leave confused but enlightened enough to tweet about it.

2. **For Group 2 (The Pragmatists):**

   It is all about **balance**. "Life is like a chakra—keep it spinning, but don't forget to pay your bills," says Baba Budget-ananda, handing out free **GST-friendly blessings.**

3. **For Group 3 (The Brand Enthusiasts):**

   Gurus lean heavily on **branding**. They launch product lines faster than influencers. Organic shampoos, spiritual fragrances, and blessed yoga mats? **Cha-ching!**

4. **For Group 4 (The Grassroots Faithful):**

   Simplicity reigns supreme. Langars, blessings for exam results, and *"Good Morning"* WhatsApp forwards do the trick. Faith in exchange for connection—no frills required.

Market Dynamics of Devotion

Let us not pretend this is not about **economics as much as enlightenment**. The spiritual market is segmented as follows:

- **Group 1:** Pays in intellectual smugness (*"I tweeted your quote; you're welcome"*).

- **Group 2:** Covers operational costs (*"Air conditioning isn't free, after all"*).

- **Group 3:** Funds the guru's **luxury SUV** (*"Blessed wheels for the blessed soul"*).

- **Group 4:** Powers the guru's private helicopter on sheer goodwill.

The Divine Irony

The beauty of this ecosystem lies in its contradictions. Rationalists wonder why spiritualists are so gullible, while spiritualists pray for the rationalists to *"open their third eye."* Meanwhile, the gurus chuckle, balancing spiritual growth with Swiss bank accounts.

And yet, in the chaos of it all, everyone comes together in the satsang hall—nodding, clapping, and chanting in unison. **Because when it comes to faith, logic takes a backseat, and devotion rides shotgun.**

India's spiritual spectrum proves one universal truth: whether you are here for the enlightenment or the free chai, there's always room for one more believer (and their wallet).

10

Horns, Harmoniums, and Honk-Happy DJs: India's Loud and Proud Symphony

India, where **sitars strum your soul**, mridangams boom with authority, and harmoniums hum like they have discovered the meaning of life, has long been the **global headquarters of melody**. Music here is not just sound; it is a way of life. From the intricate *gharanas* of classical music to Bollywood bangers that make you cry and dance simultaneously, India's musical spectrum is more expansive than a South Delhi auntie's hat collection.

But while maestros like **Ilaiyaraaja** and **AR Rahman** have taken Indian music to divine heights, an alternative soundscape has emerged from the grassroots of chaos: **the honk, the DJ remix, and the art of unholy volume.**

The Evolution of the Honk: Symphony of the Streets

It all began innocently enough—a car horn, a simple "please move" in audio form. But India, the creative powerhouse it is, could not leave it at that. Today, the car horn is not just a functional tool; it is **an instrument of self-expression**, a raag of rage, a beat of impatience, and, occasionally, a cry for help.

Horns come in a variety of tones and personalities:

- The **Gentle Peep**: A polite honk, like a soft *"Excuse me."*

- The **Persistent Buzzer**: Repeated honks, yelling, *"Move or perish!"*

- The **Turbo Tooter**: A honk so aggressive it feels like it might launch the car into orbit.

Then there are **honk virtuosos**, drivers who can turn a traffic jam into an **impromptu concert.** One beep to evaluate the waters, another to summon impatience, and then a full-on **crescendo of chaos** as every car joins the orchestra. When ten vehicles honk in unison, the sound waves can induce mild panic, clear blocked sinuses, and inspire existential questions like, *"Do I really need to go to this wedding?"*

Bangladesh's "Hooter Symphony": Why Stop at Traffic?

While Indian honkers are artists of impatience, our neighbours in **Bangladesh** have taken honking to a spiritual level. They have perfected the art of round-the-clock honking, creating a **"hooter symphony"** that echoes through alleyways, highways, and into neighbouring countries. Their motto? *"If you're awake, you should be honking."*

Whether stuck in traffic, sleeping, or eating biryani, the constant background hoots remind you of life's most important lesson: **noise is life.**

DJ Remix: The Blender of Beats

Suppose honking is the street-level soundtrack of India. In that case, **DJs are the self-appointed rockstars** of every wedding, festival, and, oddly enough, political rally. Their speciality? Turning beloved classics into something that sounds like a **kitchen appliance being tortured.**

Take a timeless melody like *"Lag Ja Gale."* Under a DJ's tender care, it becomes a high-speed anthem with so much bass that even the **ceiling fans start dancing.** Moreover, DJs in India do not just play music—they curate an experience. Every few seconds, they yell their name into the mic as if to remind you who is responsible for your eardrum damage:

- *"DJ Lala in da house!"*

- *"Bass badhao! Bass badhao!"* (Translation: "Increase the bass! Increase the bass!")

The crowd cheers, the aunties throw their hands in the air, and somewhere, a coconut tree trembles from the sheer force of sound waves.

Remake Madness: Nostalgia on Steroids

As if remixes were not enough, the **remake industry** came along to redefine what it means to "honour" a classic. Picture this: a soulful Kishore Kumar song remade with **EDM drops so loud you forget the lyrics existed.** Critics call it an insult, but fans argue it is a **modern miracle,** capable of curing boredom, nostalgia, and mild depression.

Doctors are recommending remakes to patients who lack excitement in their lives. The sudden jolt of hearing *"Aap Jaisa Koi"* with auto-tuned rap verses can stimulate adrenaline, panic, and sometimes an existential crisis.

The Holy Matrimony of Honks and DJs

For the ultimate Indian soundscape, imagine a wedding procession. The groom sits on a white horse, visibly reconsidering all his life decisions. Behind him, the **DJ's truck blasts "Kala Chashma,"** remixed with enough bass to shatter car windshields. As if that were not enough, honks from impatient drivers waiting to pass ahead add a **percussion section (Me yamla pagla deewana)** to the chaotic symphony.

This is not just music; it is **a cultural phenomenon.** The road becomes a dance floor, the bride's relatives join the traffic jam, and somewhere, a scooter weaves through, beeping its horn like it is auditioning for Indian Idol.

The Divine Art of Volume

India does not believe in subtlety, especially when it comes to sound. Whether it is a DJ remix, a political rally, or a neighbourhood Durga Puja, the volume dial is always turned to **"Are You Deaf Yet?"** Even temples and mosques get in on the action, ensuring that prayers are broadcast so loudly that even the heavens might file a noise complaint.

Market Innovation: Horns as Musical Instruments

The honk is not just noise; it is an **emerging art form.** With advancements in horn technology, we now have honks that play Bollywood tunes, patriotic anthems, and even bhajans. Who needs a radio when your car can serenade you with *"Mere Desh Ki Dharti"* every time you hit the horn?

Meanwhile, scooter manufacturers are experimenting with multi-tonal honks. Imagine honking at a traffic signal and accidentally recreating *"Chaiyya Chaiyya."* Innovation, thy name is India.

Final Movement: India's Symphony of Chaos

So, next time you are caught in traffic with horns blaring, DJs blasting, and remakes assaulting your senses, do not roll your eyes—embrace it. This is India, where **noise is culture, honks are art, and DJs are the philosophers of bass.**

In a land where the roads are raags, the DJs are the street-side Mozart, and remakes are as unpredictable as the weather, who needs subtlety anyway?

If it gets too much, just remember **it is not just sound; it is the soundtrack of a nation.** And when in doubt, carry earplugs—they might not block the noise, but they will make you feel like you are part of the solution.

From Potholes to Turbulence: The Indian Traveller's Journey

Ah, the golden days! Back when life was simpler, choices were scarce, and our only form of luxury was **idleness**. The markets were not overflowing; motorcycles came in exactly three flavours (Enfield, Yezdi, and Rajdoot), and cars were either the **chunky Ambassador**, the quirky Premier Padmini, or the adorable, tin-can-on-wheels Maruti 800. **Buses**? Tata or Ashok Leyland, their interiors lined with shiny rexine seats that doubled as sweat sponges. The roads were a patchwork of **potholes and optimism**, and a 200-kilometer journey felt like an eight-hour epic.

Buses: The OG Safar (Journey)

Inside the buses, comfort was less a feature and more of a **fantasy**. The legendary three-by-two seating arrangement offered **zero legroom and maximum thigh proximity**. Coconut-oil-coated passengers left their mark on the rexine. At the same time, the floors were wooden or metal—depending on whether the owner had a budget or just vibes. Air freshener? Only if you were not seated next to someone who treated garlic like a personality trait.

The ride quality was consistent, though—**bone-jarring** with a side of Bollywood. The driver's assistant, a jack-of-all-trades, doubled as a DJ, blasting 'nineties hits that made you feel like you were riding through a music video filmed entirely on potholes.

Stops were adventures: impromptu toilet breaks behind bushes, chai stalls with questionable hygiene, and the occasional treat of spotting a petrol pump—a true oasis in this desert of discomfort. Even the buses needed their hydration breaks, with the cleaner pouring **bucketfuls of water into the radiator** like a spa treatment for the engine.

The Flight Upgrade: From Rexine to Recline (Kind Of)

Then came aeroplanes. My first flight on a no-name airline felt like I had entered another universe. The **plush seats**, red-uniformed hosts, and pre-smartphone in-flight entertainment made my nine-year-old, pothole-jostled self-feel like royalty. They even handed out **complimentary headphones**! I floated through the clouds, blissfully unaware of the turbulence brewing in the low-cost airline industry.

Fast forward to my nonprofit-budget days, and I was firmly grounded in the world of **Air Slippers** (let us keep it cryptic, shall we?). Here, flying was less about luxury and more about survival. Boarding passes were handwritten, seats were first-come-first-served, and families scattered across the cabin clung to their seats like it was a **musical chairs championship.**

Regional Airlines: Turboprops and Turbo Chaos

Flying on regional airlines? Now, that is where the real adventure begins. Once, I escorted Latin American scientists (wearing suits in Uttarakhand's **soup-like humidity**) on a "luxury" flight from Rishikesh to Dehradun. **Baggage rules?** It is as clear as Delhi air in winter. While my guests carried twenty-five kilos of "essentials," the airline allowed only fifteen. The airport manager—bless his jugaad spirit—crafted a **Frankenstein baggage strategy**, merging hand luggage and carry-ons into an acceptable compromise.

On another flight with India's biggest airline (the one), I learned the **fine art of excess luggage fines.** Three of our bags tipped the scales by seven hundred grams, and I shelled out Rs. 1,000 per gram. By the time we boarded, I was calculating whether I could check in my soul for extra savings.

Blue Air: The Bus of the Skies

And then there's **Blue Air** (again, no names—just clues). Blue Air is the final boss level if buses were the training ground for discomfort. They have turned passengers into unpaid clerks: you print your boarding pass, tag your luggage, and practically assemble your seat. Once aboard, you realise the **3x2 bus seats** were La-Z-Boys compared to Blue Air's wafer-thin cushions.

Legroom? A myth. Reclining? Forbidden. If you are lucky, turbulence might lean your seat back for you. The lavatories? About as spacious as a **clothes dryer**. But do not worry—they make up for what they lack in comfort by strictly enforcing the **7-kilo hand luggage rule.**

The Culinary Carnival: From Cardboard to Pebbles

Airplane food deserves its own Netflix special. These "delicacies" include:

- **Upma** with the consistency of packing peanuts.

- **Poha** that crunches like gravel.

- **Noodles** so dry they could pass for dehydrated worms.

And let us not forget the **water policy**: hydration is sold in eyedropper portions, ensuring you stay thirsty enough to buy another bottle. Alcohol? The menu claims it is available but as elusive as **legroom in economy class.**

The In-Flight Drama: Where Rules Rule Supreme

In-flight arguments are where true comedy unfolds. On one trip, a **Delhi diva** launched into an enthusiastic Hinglish debate over her luggage's karmic balance:

- *"Last time, na, I carried less. So, this time, it evens out, okay?"*

The cabin crew's unyielding reply? *"Madam, rules are rules."*

The result? A standoff is as epic as a soap opera climax.

From Potholes to Turbulence: The Unchanged Essence

Whether by bus or aeroplane, travelling in India always carries a touch of **chaotic charm.** The only difference is the altitude—your bones rattled on the ground are now lightly shaken at 30,000 feet. But at least with turbulence, no cleaner water is poured into the plane's engine.

For all its quirks, each journey adds a chapter to your travel diary, whether it is squeezing into a minimalist airline seat or surviving a bus ride that feels like an eight-hour audition for a **spinal endurance contest.** Because here in India, the journey is less about comfort and more about the stories you will tell later—after you have recovered.

12

Sky-High Irony: The Chronicles of Middle-Class Flying

Picture this: India's burgeoning middle class—champions of frugality, collectors of EMI dreams, and weekend trip planners extraordinaire—has embraced the joys of **"budget" flying.** It is called "no-frills airlines" because the only thing Indian travellers love more than saving money is suffering for it. Why enjoy a reclining seat with a meal when you can squeeze into a plastic throne and pay ₹300 for a samosa that tastes like crushed ambition?

The Prelude: Airports—Where Common Sense Goes to Die

Before you even board the plane, the drama begins at the airport. Airports are no longer gateways, but capitalist utopias disguised as transportation hubs. **Want water?** ₹50 for a bottle you could have refilled at home for free. **Biscuits?** A humble ₹10 pack of Parle-G gets a designer price tag of ₹150.

For the bold and slightly masochistic, there's airport food. A dosa that costs ₹80 at a roadside Udupi joint is suddenly ₹**450**, and no, it does not come with sambhar refills—it comes with regret. Fancy a coffee? That is

₹**250** for what tastes like last night's leftover instant brew reheated in a jet engine.

But here is the kicker: the middle class **willingly partakes** in this airport carnival of extortion. **"We're at the airport!"** they declare as if that justifies spending the equivalent of a Netflix subscription on a sandwich.

The Budget Airline Hustle

You board the no-frills airline, still clutching your overpriced dosa crumbs, and settle into a seat as forgiving as a Delhi summer. The air host flashes a polite smile—her training manual clearly instructed her to smile through existential despair—and hands you the **madness menu.**

A bottle of water, priced at ₹50 downstairs, is now a **sky-high ₹100.** A vada pav, Mumbai's beloved street snack, is priced at ₹**300**, and no, there is no chutney—it comes wrapped in plastic and served with a side of heartbreak.

But the true pièce de résistance is the ₹**200 samosa.** Not a gourmet samosa, mind you—just a sad, soggy triangle that has been reheated more than the airline's safety drills. **And yet, people buy it.** Why? Because the shame of admitting you forgot snacks at home is greater than the pain of a ₹200 samosa.

The Gulf Labourer's Plight

Now, let us shift to a different aisle—one occupied by a Gulf labourer returning home after years of hard labour. He earned every dirham through sweat, saving every penny for his family. But the airport economy mocks his thrift.

At Gulf airports, **water costs ₹300.** A simple meal? ₹1,000. The labourer looks at the menu, calculates his wallet's endurance, and chooses hunger over bankruptcy. When he boards the no-frills airline, the menu is no kinder. ₹300 for Vada pav or ₹300 for his child's school fees? He chooses the latter, takes a sip from his water bottle filled before departure, and swallows his pride.

The Seating Circus

Meanwhile, our middle-class passengers are busy convincing themselves they are living the dream. Sure, the legroom is a joke, and reclining your seat is about as controversial as the Indian Parliament, but **"At least we're flying!"** they proclaim, ignoring that train travel could have been cheaper and comfier and came with samosas included.

First-timers bring a unique brand of chaos. The overhead bins? Stuffed with everything except what they need. The seatbelt? A mystery they fumble with for a solid 10 minutes. And do not even mention the in-flight toilet—a labyrinth of buttons and knobs that leaves them wondering if flushing might accidentally eject them mid-air.

The "Premium" Scam

Then there is the **"premium seat" upgrade,** a marketing miracle that convinces passengers to pay ₹1,000 extra for a window seat near the wing—where the only view is a scratched window and the occasional oil stain. Premium? Sure, if you consider proximity to the screaming engine a luxury.

The Apathy of It All

What is truly shocking is how **normalised** this absurdity has become. Airlines justify their pricing with fancy phrases like **"operational costs,"** while airports monetise every necessity. And the middle class? They wear their suffering like a badge of honour. **"Do you know I paid ₹700 for a dosa at the airport? So posh!"** they brag, conveniently forgetting the tears they shed while eating it.

The Flying Irony

No-frills airlines are supposed to make air travel affordable, but they are just a parody of themselves. They have turned flying into an airborne extortion racket, where even the air feels more expensive.

The **vada pav** costs ₹300. The chai tastes like sadness. And the seat? It is a masterclass in minimalism—minimal comfort, minimal space, and maximum regret.

Conclusion: Pack Snacks and Pray for Sanity

Flying no-frills in India is not just travel but a **psychological experiment.** It evaluates how much discomfort, overpricing, and indignity the average Indian can endure in the name of saving money. So next time you book that budget ticket, remember: the real luxury is not the flight—the samosa you packed from home.

Welcome to the skies, where the irony soars higher than the planes.

13

The Great Airplane Huddle: Chaos in the Skies, Grounded on Earth

As the plane descends onto Delhi Airport's tarmac, passengers sit in quiet anticipation— or rather, the *illusion* of quiet. The second the seatbelt sign dims; the cabin erupts into **pandemonium**. The flight attendants' gentle reminder to "stay seated until the aircraft comes to a complete stop" is met with all the respect of a cat ignoring its owner.

It is not disobedience; it is tradition. This is the **Indian Grand Prix**, the sacred ritual of **who can get off first**, complete with elbows, overstuffed bags, and footwork that could rival a Bollywood dance-off.

The Human Tetris Begins

The aisles quickly become a **battleground of limbs**, bags, and fragile egos. Passengers, packed together tighter than **parathas in a tiffin box**, contort their bodies into shapes that would make yoga instructors proud. **Tall passengers fold themselves like human accordions**, bending in ways that defy logic and anatomy.

Meanwhile, the overhead compartments become **gravity's playground**, with bags teetering dangerously close to launching a **duty-free disaster**. A bottle of imported whiskey wobbles ominously, threatening to become the most expensive puddle in aviation history.

And then, with all the grace of a stampede at a Bollywood premiere, the **aisle sprint begins**.

The Race to the Exit: Survival of the Quickest

As the gate opens, it is a chaotic situation. The sprinters at the front charge forward with the **determination of Delhi uncles at a wedding buffet**, armed with trolley bags that double as battering rams. A seasoned traveller elbows ahead, executing Kabaddi moves with surgical precision.

Behind him, a woman with a handbag the size of Haryana **bulldozes through like a freight train**, her mission clear: **be the first to the bus.** In her wake, a middle-aged man, clutching a bag stuffed with at least one illegal quantity of mangoes, mutters, *"Yeh log kaunse sanskaar leke aaye hain?"* (Translation: "Where are their manners?").

The Overachievers: Already Standing at Take-off

Then there are the **overachiever**s who stood up the second the wheels kissed the tarmac. They have mastered the art of balancing precariously in the aisle, resembling flamingos on a tightrope, while clutching bags, scarves, and at least one forgotten neck pillow. Their faces beam with triumph as if **being vertical first guarantees a better seat on the bus.**

Little do they know this victory is as short-lived as their patience.

The Hippies and the Wisemen: Chaos, Who?

And then, amidst the chaos, there is **the Zen group**: the Hippies and the Wisemen. These enlightened souls sit calmly, legs crossed, expressions serene, watching the chaos unfold like an episode of *Koffee with Karan*. Their mantra:

"Why rush? The bus is not leaving without us, and neither is enlightenment."

They rise with the elegance of a lotus blooming in slow motion, stretching, adjusting their bags, and taking selfies. Their secret weapon? **Patience and the ability to bend time.**

The Bus Shuffle: Where Legends Are Born

As everyone finally funnels into the shuttle bus, the sprinting champions find themselves squashed at the back, wedged between someone's duffel bag and a particularly aggressive auntie demanding the driver turn on the AC. Meanwhile, the **Zen group glides on board last**, securing the **prime spot by the doors.**

It is **traffic karma in action.**

When the bus halts at the terminal, the sprinters—once smug with victory—now resemble sardines trying to escape their tin. The Zen group, on the other hand, steps off first, throwing a knowing smile at the chaos they left behind. Somewhere, a sitar plays softly, and the universe nods in approval.

The Luggage Carousel: Round Two

But the saga does not end there. At the luggage carousel, **another race begins**. The same sprinters—now fuelled by frustration—station themselves directly at the mouth of the conveyor belt, creating a human barricade that makes retrieving bags a game of **dodge and grab.**

Overzealous uncles shove past, yelling, *"Arre, woh mera bag hai!"* (Translation: "Hey, that's my bag!") at every piece of luggage that remotely resembles theirs. Meanwhile, a traveller who clearly has not packed in decades tries to **yank someone else's suitcase** because *"sab black bag lagte hain."* (Translation: "All black bags look the same.")

The Zen group? Still unfazed. They stand at the edge of the chaos, sipping overpriced coffee and occasionally nodding at their luggage as if to say, *"Take your time; we'll be here."*

The Ride Home: Chaos on the Ground

As the journey continues, the sprinters compete for the best cab, negotiating with drivers who clearly enjoy quoting **"peak pricing."** An argument breaks out over **Rs. 50**, and someone screams, *"Bhaiya, Google Maps on karo na!"* (Translation: "Brother, just turn on Google Maps!").

The Zen group? They have already booked their cab, pre-paid online, and are halfway home, meditating on the meaning of turbulence.

The Moral of the Madness

The Great Airplane Huddle is more than just a journey—it is a **microcosm of India's unfiltered spirit.** It is chaotic, loud, and occasionally bruising but also hilariously entertaining.

For every sprinter fighting for the aisle, a Zen master is waiting to outwit them with calm. For every overhead bag waiting to fall, a hopeful traveller thinks, *"Maybe this time, the aisle will be clear."*

And while the bus-to-terminal shuffle feels like **purgatory on wheels**, it reminds us that travel is never about getting there in India. It is a full-contact sport, a test of patience, and a story you will retell every time you book a flight.

Because in the end, whether you are a sprinter or a Zen master, one thing is sure: **Delhi Airport is where legends are made, and sanity is left at baggage claim.**

14

Gender Transformation and Changing Mindsets in India: A Tale of Schemes, Scams, and Sarees

In a country where job exams are a cruel cocktail of **talent, endurance, and sheer bureaucratic chaos**, unemployed male youth are losing their patience—and their marbles. Paper leaks? Like clockwork. Exam postponements? As regular as tea breaks. A job ratio of **1:1 million**? Of course. And just to rub salt in the wound, PhD holders are mopping floors in government offices because **why dream big when you can sweep big?**

But Indian youth are nothing if not innovative. When life traps them in the **unemployment chakravyuh**, they do what they do best: **jugaad.**

The Eureka Moment: The "Unemployed Youth Congress" Revolution

Tired of rejections and ridicule, a group of unemployed warriors convened at a secret chai stall for the **Unemployed Youth Congress** (no political affiliation, though you would not guess). Over half a packet of

Parle-G, they brainstormed strategies to beat the system that had failed them. And then came the masterstroke:

Exploit the women-centric freebies!

Their **grand plan**? Apply en masse for free gender-affirming procedures under women empowerment schemes.

"If we can't beat the system as men, let's join it as women," declared Raju, an MA in Physics whose closest interaction with physics now involves calculating how to survive on a government stipend of zero rupees.

The Benefits: One Stone, Many Birds

1. **Government Jobs Galore:** As freshly minted women, they would qualify for all the **women-only job quotas**, sidestepping half the competition. Why fight with one million desperate men when you can enter a job designed for Ghar Ki Lakshmi?

2. **Improved Gender Ratios:** Haryana and Bundelkhand, notorious for their skewed gender ratios, would finally see an influx of eligible "brides." Said Rinku, "Nothing screams 'better future' like fixing Haryana's marriage crisis one operation at a time!"

3. **Family Pride Restored:** Sons labelled failures for not securing a government job would now be celebrated as **hardworking daughters.** "Better to be Beti Raju with a scheme-sponsored sewing machine than Beta Raju with nothing but shame," quipped one young visionary.

4. **Dowry Drama Flipped:** Families of these "new daughters" would now **receive dowry** instead of paying it. Imagine the irony: unemployed youth turning into financial assets with one well-timed operation.

Breaking Stereotypes: The Gender Revolution Begins

Youth across states are lining up at government hospitals with newfound hope. "Unlike that Algerian boxer who refused to change her gender for Olympic glory, we have no such hang-ups," said Shyam, a B. Tech graduate who dreams of running a **self-help group (SHG)**.

"Four years of Agniveer service or a lifetime of sarees, LPG connections, and reserved jobs? Easy choice," he added, already Googling "best saree pleats for beginners."

Parents, too, are on board. *Mera beta… sorry, meri beti ab IAS banegi!*" one teary-eyed mother exclaimed, clutching her son's—oops, daughter's—hand as they filled out the paperwork. Another mother said, "With the free LPG from Ujjwala Yojana, our new daughter can finally learn how to cook. It is all falling into place!"

Haryana: The Dream Destination

If this gender revolution has a capital, it is **Haryana**, where the scarcity of women has created a booming "bride economy." Transformed men are receiving marriage proposals faster than job offers.

"First, naukri nahi mili (could not get a job); now, pati mil gaya (got a husband). Life is full of surprises," quipped Chintu, now Chandni, who recently accepted a proposal from a 40-year-old Jat farmer. Her dowry? **A brand-new tractor.**

Critics, Concerns, and Confusion

Of course, not everyone is clapping. Feminists are raising eyebrows, arguing that these "transformed men" are unfairly **hijacking privileges meant for actual women.** Bureaucrats, meanwhile, are scratching their heads, trying to make sense of the sudden spike in gender reassignment requests.

When questioned about adapting to their new roles, the youth laughed. "We have been juggling unemployment, societal pressure, and family shame for years. **Multitasking is in our blood.** Running a household and a job? Easy."

The Unintended Side Effects

As with any grand social experiment, unintended side effects abound:

- **New Social Norms:** Young men-now-women are navigating **bride-selection ceremonies**, adjusting to the art of rejecting unsuitable grooms.

- **Fashion Disasters:** Saree pleats and eyeliner mishaps are rampant, but YouTube tutorials are bridging the gap.

- **Community Confusion:** Matchmakers are scrambling to adapt. One was overheard lamenting, "Do I ask for height and complexion or their **previous gender's profession?**"

A Glorious Future (and a Dose of Irony)

As thousands of young men transform into women under government schemes, India finds itself at the forefront of an **unintended social experiment**. Gender parity improves, unemployment drops, and dowries—ironically—fuel financial stability for families.

Because in India, when life shuts a door, we **build a new one**, repaint it, and turn it into a scheme. And if that does not work, we change genders, pick up a sewing machine, and become the **daughter of the house.**

So next time you hear someone sigh, "Yeh desh ka kuch nahi ho sakta" (This country has no hope), remind them:

In India, when unemployment hits hard, innovation hits harder—sometimes in a saree and bangles.

15

The Great Convenience Hypocrisy: Our Selective Outrage Circus

Ah, **convenience**—the backbone of modern life and the golden chariot of hypocrisy. Nowhere is this paradox more gloriously evident than in the buzzing virtual classrooms of **WhatsApp University**. Here, professors (read: uncles and aunties) and their overzealous "students" dispense revolutionary insights while munching samosas and sipping chai. Forget Ivy League rigour—this is where intellectual gymnastics happen, fueled by unverified forwards and unlimited free time.

Lesson One: The Common Enemy Curriculum

The cornerstone of WhatsApp University? The sacred art of **hating a common enemy.** Why do we hate Country A or Group B? The reasons are as solid as a papad during monsoon.

Professor Uncle begins: *"Why do we hate Country A?"*

Student Bhola, mid-bite of his samosa, replies confidently: *"Because they support Country B!"*

Uncle nods sagely and continues: *"And why do we hate Country B?"*

Auntie Kavita, sipping tea from her *"Live, Laugh, Love"* mug, chimes in: *"Because they exist."*

None of them have ever visited these countries or know anyone from there. But who needs facts when **WhatsApp forwards** have already confirmed that Country B invented traffic jams, global warming, and your neighbour's noisy dog?

The Western World Paradox

Nowhere is our hypocrisy shinier than in our love-hate relationship with the **Western world.** We passionately denounce their *"decadent lifestyle"* while simultaneously clinging to their products like a lifeline.

Uncle Chaturvedi rants about the **evils of Western influence**, updating his Facebook status from his **iPhone** while sipping **Coca-Cola.** *"These Westerners have ruined our culture!"* he declares, in between bites of **Italian pasta.** Auntie Meera nods in agreement, adjusting her **Ray-Ban sunglasses**, and says, *"But did you see their Black Friday sales?"*

And when it comes to **defending the nation**, the irony hits Mach 5:

"We must defeat the enemy!" bellows WhatsApp Professor Pandey.

"With what?" asks a naive student.

"Western technology, of course!" Pandey thunders, proudly pointing to a missile marked **"Made in the USA."**

Conveniently Inconvenient Truths

Our hypocrisy shines brightest when we address "moral issues" with the flexibility of a yoga instructor:

Dressing of Women

Auntie Kavita, in her **designer salwar kameez**, lectures her niece about wearing jeans:

"This is why our culture is in danger!" she huffs. Minutes later, she is drooling over her favourite Bollywood actor in a **miniskirt**, calling her *"modern and graceful."*

Food Rituals

Uncle Rana devours bread omelette like it is his life's mission but condemns his neighbour for eating red meat. *"It's about sanctity,"* he insists, sipping chicken gravy soup off his fingers with zero irony.

Killing Animals

Killing animals is perfectly acceptable—if it is done *"our way."* Auntie Madhu protests certain rituals but gleefully orders **mutton biryani**. *"This is different,"* she explains without further clarification, and none is ever needed.

God, Technology, and Divine Hypocrisy

We proudly use technology to "prove" God's greatness while dismissing the science behind it. Dean Mishra declares: *"God created everything!"* while typing furiously on a laptop powered by **decades of human innovation.**

"Animals don't follow religion," pipes up a brave student.

"Exactly! That is why they are inferior!" snaps Mishra. He conveniently ignores the fact that animals do not start wars over temples, mosques, or which direction to pray. Nor do they argue about whether their burrows are Vastu-compliant.

Blood, Organs, and the Ultimate Irony

If there is one place where hypocrisy truly shines, it is the **hospital.** All prejudices vanish faster than the promises of a politician post-election.

"Doctor Saab, whose blood is this?" someone asks tensely.

"It's from someone you despise," the doctor replies.

"Oh, okay. Just make sure it is O positive."

At that moment, caste, religion, and nationality dissolve like sugar in chai. The organs that save lives come from the people we criticise during dinner conversations.

The Hypocrisy Olympics: Gold Medal Performances

We have mastered selective outrage, competing fiercely in the **Hypocrisy Olympics:**

- **Polygamy:** *"It's barbaric!"* we cry, forgetting our own history of kings with harems larger than football teams.

- **Veils:** *"Why oppress women?"* someone yells while pointing fingers at others, conveniently ignoring their own cultural practices.

- **Morality:** *"We're a moral nation!"* we declare while watching pirated movies and dodging taxes like seasoned pros.

The Final Lesson: Selective Ignorance is Bliss

The hallmark of our hypocrisy? **Never admit it.** While animals roam blissfully unaware of religion, politics, or WhatsApp forwards, we pride ourselves on being "higher beings" who can create wars over **imaginary enemies and invisible boundaries.**

Because let us be honest: **God did not create hypocrisy—we did.** And we have been perfecting it ever since, one forwarded message and contradictory rant at a time.

Convenience Over Conscience

So, the next time Uncle Sharma lectures you on morality while sipping imported scotch or Auntie Kavita denounces Western culture from her air-conditioned living room, remember:

Convenience is king.

Our collective hypocrisy is less about what we believe and more about what is convenient. After all, why wrestle with inconvenient truths when you can enjoy a **butter chicken-fueled rant about values,** all while shopping on Amazon during a Black Friday sale?

Because in India, if life is a circus, hypocrisy is the ringmaster, and convenience is the showstopper act.

16

The Great Indian Security Ballet: Guards, Bribes, and Polyester Dreams

In the chaotic orchestra of Delhi's society, where every bungalow, mall, and barely functioning ATM demands its own **security guard**, an entire subculture thrives in polyester uniforms and weary sighs. These unsung sentinels of the city stand at the intersection of **comedy and tragedy**, juggling societal indifference, existential dread, and the occasional bribe.

Welcome to the Guard Room: A Luxury-Free Zone

Every Delhi bungalow has a **guard room**—a euphemism for a cupboard-sized purgatory where guards sit or rather crouch on plastic chairs that double as medieval torture instruments. The "room" is typically equipped with:

- A fan (functional only when the electricity gods feel generous).

- A mug that moonlights as a teacup, a mosquito trap, and sometimes, a cricket trophy.

Ram Kishore, a 62-year-old guard, sums it up best: *"Retirement? That is for the bungalow owners. For us, it is just a fancy word for unemployment."*

He spends his 12-hour shifts between saluting residents and scaring off street dogs, all while mentally composing poetry about hunger and rent.

The Mall Guards: Polyester with Pomp

Malls have their own breed of guards—armed with **metal detectors that beep for everything except actual metal.** Their primary role is confiscating water bottles and wielding their authority like a family heirloom.

- A young couple tries to sneak in a half-empty bottle of water.

- *Beep!* The guard frowns with an intensity worthy of a Bollywood villain. *"Paani andar allowed nahi hai."* (Water is not allowed inside.)

- Meanwhile, a Bentley pulls up. A quick ₹500 exchange later, the tinted windows glide through, parking illegally yet elegantly.

Hotels and Airports: A Tale of Two Cities

In Delhi's five-star hotels, guards are experts in **selective politeness:**

- A foreign tourist receives a warm *"Welcome, sir!"*

- Meanwhile, an uncle in a kurta asking for the washroom gets the kind of look usually reserved for tax evaders.

At airports, the guards have perfected *"The Nod"*—a subtle gesture that can mean anything from *"You're good to go"* to *"I'm bored, let's open your bag."* Officers, on the other hand, turn bribe solicitation into an art form.

- *"Sir, your imported cheese exceeds the limit."*

- *"What's the fine?"*

- *"₹2,000… or ₹1,500 if you wink right now."*

Night Shifts and Existential Crises

For guards working night shifts, life is a blur of hunger, sleep deprivation, and barking at delivery boys. Raju, a veteran of the trade, shares his survival strategy: *"Double shifts are great—I'm too tired to feel hungry and too broke to eat."*

By night, he dreams of a life where he is not saluting teenagers revving their bikes like Formula 1 racers. By day, he confronts furious residents yelling about leaves falling on their driveways.

The Police: Guards with Extra Swagger

On a slightly higher rung are the **Delhi Police**, experts in **negotiation**.

- You jump a red light, and the officer adjusts his cap dramatically.

- *"Chalaan toh ₹2,000 ka hai... par aap samajhdaar lagte ho."* (The fine is ₹2,000, but you seem reasonable.)

- Translation: "Let's settle this over chai money."

Empathy? What's That?

Society's treatment of guards is a masterclass in apathy. Residents yell about guards taking tea breaks, blissfully ignoring that those breaks are the only sustenance guards have between shifts.

Hari Ram, a septuagenarian guard, puts it bluntly: *"Who needs knees when ₹5,000 a month keeps you alive?"* He starts his shift at 8 PM and ends when the bungalow owner wants to wake up.

Guards vs. Upper Management: Polyester vs. Rolex

In private security firms, the bosses sit in **air-conditioned offices**, sipping artisanal coffee while giving TED Talk-worthy speeches about teamwork.

- *"Our guards are the backbone of our company,"* says one manager, adjusting his Rolex.

- *"We pay them enough to keep their backs from breaking."*

Meanwhile, the guards survive on hope, borrowed samosas, and the occasional unsolicited lecture from residents about "working harder."

Guardroom Philosophers: Life Lessons in Polyester

Guards have evolved into philosophers, pondering life's more profound questions between salutes.

- *"Why do I guard a bungalow I can't afford to rent the garage of?"*

- *"If a leaf falls and the guard doesn't sweep it, does it matter?"*

- *"How much chai is too much chai?"*

Ram Kishore reflects: *"We are not just guards. We are observers of life. The world moves on while we stand still—literally."*

A Tragicomic Dance

Delhi's guards perform a daily **ballet of endurance, apathy, and polyester uniforms**. Whether it is mall security confiscating water bottles, bungalow guards surviving on chai fumes, or airport customs officers turning bribes into performance art, they are the unsung heroes of a society that notices them only when they are gone.

As Ram Kishore puts it: *"We are guards, not gods. But sometimes, it feels like we are guarding life itself—with a plastic chair and sheer willpower."*

And so, the great **Indian Security Ballet** continues—a tragicomic dance of low pay, high endurance, and unacknowledged dignity. But hey, at least they have their guardrooms… and chai.

17

The Great Indian Highway Chronicles: A Dhaba Drama for the Ages

The Indian highway is not just a road; it is an adventure waiting to happen—a soap opera played out on stretches of asphalt. At the heart of this drama is the **Vaishno Dhabas**, the chaotic yet oddly charming eateries that promise **soul food with a side of daylight robbery**.

Murthal Beginnings: A Family's Pit Stop

It was supposed to be a straightforward road trip from Delhi to Chandigarh. My family, armed with snacks, playlists, and an overly optimistic ETA, had barely crossed the Delhi border when hunger struck.

Enter **Murthal**, the mecca of dhabas. As we pulled into a sprawling Vaishno Dhaba with neon lights brighter than an IPL stadium, my dad declared, *"Yeh asli highway experience, hai!"* (This is the real highway experience!).

Inside, the air buzzed with activity. Waiters balanced towering trays of parathas, families squabbled over chutney bowls, and a group of uncles discreetly sipped something "special" behind a parked truck. The menu boasted **butter-loaded parathas, dal tadka, and khichdi** that promised comfort but delivered chaos.

₹350 for khichdi?" my mom gasped. *"Yeh toh gold-plated honi chahiye!"* (It should be gold-plated for this price!). The food arrived, swimming in enough ghee to drown a small village, and we dug in. It was not terrible, but for ₹250, I expected my dal to at least **wave at a lentil**.

As we left, my dad muttered: *"Next time, simple roti sabzi."* A promise he would conveniently forget at the next dhaba.

Rajasthan's Chili Roulette

The road to Jodhpur brought us to a **Rajasthani dhaba** perched by the highway, looking innocent enough—until the food arrived. The sabzi was chilli **paste masquerading as curry**, and even the **chaas** (buttermilk) carried a suspicious kick.

One bite in, and my tongue was ablaze. Brave but foolish brother declared: *"Kuch nahi hota, it's all in the mind."* (It is all mental). Seconds later, he was gulping water like a man stranded in the desert.

The dhaba owner, unfazed, handed us tissues for our tears and said: *"Rajasthan ka swaad hai, bhaiya."* (This is the taste of Rajasthan). Taste? More like **a gastronomic assault**.

The Vaishno Clones and the Bus Mafia

By the time we reached Madhya Pradesh, the landscape had become an endless loop of **Vaishno Dhabas**, each claiming to be "original."

- *"New Original Vaishno Dhaba."*

- *"Super Shudh Vaishno Dhaba."*

- *"The Authentic Vaishno Delight."*

We stopped at one, lured by the promise of "authenticity." The food was okay—parathas, dal, and a surprisingly good lassi—but the bill made us question our life choices. **₹50 for papad?** Who knew inflation affected crispy lentil discs, too?

Worse still, the bus mafia was in full swing. A private bus rolled in, and passengers were herded inside like sheep. A simple roti-sabzi meal set them back ₹500 per head while the driver enjoyed his **free mutton curry**.

The Toilets: A Post-Apocalyptic Scene

No dhaba journey is complete without the **toilet challenge**. Each stop brought a new horror story. At one, the tap dripped like a countdown to your demise, the flush was missing, and the smell—oh, the scent—could have been weaponised.

My dad emerged pale but triumphant, declaring: *"Ek din ke liye toh sab adjust karna padta hai."* (You must adjust for a day). Easy for him to say—he did not have to step into the biohazard zone twice.

Snacks, Maggi, and Ayurvedic Miracles

Every dhaba had a **snack counter** selling dubious Ayurvedic powders alongside churan (digestive aids). One product, **"Swasth Jeevan Churan"** (Healthy Life Powder), claimed to cure everything from gas to heartbreak. My mom bought a packet for the laughs; my dad secretly tried it.

Meanwhile, **Maggi**, the universal highway staple, was reinvented at every stop. We encountered:

- **Paneer Maggi** (surprisingly edible).

- **Cola Maggi** (a crime against humanity).

- **Sweet Maggi** (milk, sugar, and childhood trauma in a bowl).

The Unexpected Silver Lining

Not all dhabas are frauds in disguise. Somewhere near Uttarakhand, we stumbled upon a gem. The parathas were fresh, the lassi heavenly, and the owner refused payment for the **baby food** we requested for my niece.

- *"Highway pe toh insaniyat zaroori hai,"* (Humanity is essential on highways) he said with a smile. For a moment, faith in humanity was restored.

The Highway: A Stage for Shenanigans

The highway added to the drama as we rolled toward our destination.

- Toll booths every thirty kilometres evaluated our patience. *"Fastag hai, fast nahi,"* (Fastag is not fast) my dad grumbled.

- Drivers zigzagged across lanes like they were auditioning for an action movie.

- VIP motorcades breezed past us, sirens blaring because rules clearly do not apply to important people.

The End of the Road

When we reached Chandigarh, we were exhausted, lighter by several thousand rupees, and filled with stories of overpriced parathas, fiery chillies, and post-apocalyptic toilets.

As my dad parked the car, he declared: *"Next time, we'll pack food from home."*

We all nodded, knowing we would be sitting in another dhaba soon, debating the merits of ₹**350 khichdi** and braving the **Great Indian Highway Chronicles** once again.

Because in India, a road trip is not just about the destination—it is about the chaos, the comedy, and the culinary crimes you survive along the way.

18

Big Buildings, Bigger Burdens: Dreams on a Foundation of Dust

Welcome to **Dreamville Society**, where every brick whispers irony, and the cement smells faintly of hypocrisy. Here, luxury flats rise majestically toward the heavens. At the same time, the very workers who build them remain firmly planted in **dystopian purgatory** as if gravity itself will not let them aspire for more.

Luxury by Day, Despair by Night

By day, these workers transform dusty plots into **architectural marvels** featuring infinity pools, bright lighting, and closets more oversized than their shanties. By night, they retreat to skeletal structures that resemble set designs for a post-apocalyptic film.

Picture this: A family of five living in what will someday be a "penthouse with a view." However, their only view is of **brick piles, half-dug trenches**, and mosquitoes auditioning for *Jaws: The Insect Edition*. A toddler plays joyfully with rusted nails, believing them action figures. At the same time, his mother flips chapatis on a tin sheet stove, her culinary genius wasted on a flame that threatens to extinguish with every gust of wind.

Morning Auditions: India's Got Labor

A dusty square transforms into the labour market at dawn. This scene combines the energy of *Indian Idol* with the heartbreak of a **budget reality show**. Contractors arrive in rickety cars, looking more like debt collectors than job providers.

"Too skinny? Next!"

"Got a limp? Try begging, not lifting!"

"Speak Hindi fluently? Great, now climb that scaffold with no safety harness!"

It is brutal yet comedic. The ones who are "hired" become **contestants in the Hunger Games**, except here, the arena is made of cement and rebar, and the only prize is **survival till payday**.

The Death-Defying Workday

The chosen few start their 12-hour shift with **death-defying stunts** on precarious scaffolding. Safety gear? Ha! The closest thing to a helmet is the plastic bucket they wear to shield themselves from falling debris. A fever? Here is some cement dust for flavour. Sprained ankle? **Walk it off, champ!**

If Bollywood made a movie about these labourers, it would be titled *Lagaan 2: Building Dreams with Broken Backs*. Except, there is no Aamir Khan, just contractors yelling, "**Aur tez kaam karo!**" (Work faster!)

The SUV Brigade: Inspecting Dreams from a Distance

Meanwhile, future flat owners will arrive in shiny SUVs, with their air conditioning set to "arctic." They tiptoe across the construction site, their shoes worth more than a labourer's monthly wage, clutching **designer handkerchiefs** to block the "stench of poverty."

"What's that smell?" one asks, wrinkling their nose. (Spoiler: It is their conscience decaying rapidly.)

They glance at the workers and mutter, **"Such filth, they don't even clean up after themselves,"** while casually tossing their latte cups onto the rubble.

Contrasts in Dreams and Drinks

Upstairs, these would-be owners sip cocktails and discuss **feng shui**, marble finishes, and **chandeliers that scream opulence**. Downstairs, the workers sip water from dented steel cups, dreaming of chai that does not taste like boiled despair.

For the wealthy, the **idea of a bar** involves fine whiskeys. A "bar" is the local liquor shack for the labourers, where cheap country liquor is consumed like its **liquid courage** for another day of indignities.

The Children: Abstract Artists in Dust

While the parents labour, their children create **abstract art** on unfinished walls, using sticks to draw lines that could rival a modern art exhibit. They dream of school but settle for lessons in **dodging falling bricks** and inhaling dust like pros.

Their curriculum includes:

- **How to Survive Without Shoes**

- **Advanced Techniques in Mosquito Negotiation**

- **Brick Balancing for Beginners**

Contractors: the antagonists

The real antagonists of this dramedy are the **contractors**, who operate with the charm of Bollywood villains but with polyester shirts instead of leather jackets. Their motivational speeches include gems like:

- **"Kaam karna hai toh karo, warna aur log mil jayenge."** (Work if you want; there are plenty more where you came from.)

- **"Injury ka chhutti? Pichle janam ka hisaab ab le rahe ho kya?"** (Injury leave? Are you settling scores from your past life?)

The Comedy of Inspection

The flat owners conduct **monthly inspection tours**, squinting at every detail like amateur detectives. "The marble isn't shiny enough," complains one. Another demands a **jacuzzi**, claiming, "A home without a jacuzzi is like chai without masala!"

Meanwhile, the labourers' idea of a luxury bath involves finding a **working water pump**.

The Ironic Conclusion

As the sun sets, the SUV brigade drives off, their dreams of **perfect living rooms and massive chandeliers** intact. The labourers retire to makeshift homes, eating meagre dinners under flickering bulbs. They dream not of opulence but of **a future where their children do not have to break bricks to break bread**.

Somewhere in the rubble, a mosquito buzzes approvingly as if to say, **"Even I live better than you."**

Under Construction, Forever

The flats will be completed. The wealthy will sip champagne in their infinity pools, marvelling at their good fortune. However, for the labourers who built them, their dreams remain **stuck in scaffolding**, caught between the first and second floors of a society that forgot to build a foundation for them.

Because in **Dreamville Society**, the only thing rising faster than the buildings is the **weight of irony.**

19

The Great Indian Education Circus: A Tale of Public Misnomers and International Illusions

Once upon a time, an education system that could rival Shakespearean comedies in irony and Kafkaesque tales in absurdity thrived in the land of paradoxes. Here, the words "public" and "international" were thrown around with reckless abandon, much like **India's traffic rules (or the knowledge of it)**. Welcome to the saga of Indian schools—where reality and branding rarely shake hands, but hilarity? That is always in session.

Public Schools: Where the Public is Missing

Ah, Indian public schools! The name itself deserves a **Nobel Prize for Misleading Nomenclature**. Globally, public goods are accessible to all—parks, libraries, and even stray cricket matches in open fields. But Indian "public" schools? They are as exclusive as private islands, and the entry fee could finance a medium-sized Bollywood movie.

Take their fee structure:

- **Tuition fee**: A small fortune.

- **Development fee**: This is obviously for expanding the principal's office.

- **The extracurricular fee** covers three footballs and a skipping rope for the year.

And the names? They are a delightful cocktail of **spiritual aspiration and plagiarism**:

- *Vivekananda Global Wisdom Institute*: A tribute to the monk, minus his vow of simplicity.

- *Tagore Zenith Academy International*: Because why stop at one cultural icon?

The only thing "public" about these schools is their ability to publicly shame parents at PTMs for not contributing enough to the annual *Diya* decoration drive.

International Schools: Where Global Dreams Meet Local Realities

Now, let us talk about **"international" schools**, the crown jewels of modern Indian education. The term "international" here is used with the same creative license as a Bollywood plot twist.

What is international, you ask?

- The air-conditioning in the principal's cabin was imported from Singapore.

- The football turf is so advanced that no one can step on it.

- The curriculum is where students learn French from a teacher who says *"merci"* like it rhymes with "fancy."

Parents line up for admissions, not for their kids' merit but for their own **"brag rights."** PTA meetings feel like **reality show auditions**, with parents flaunting their vacation photos, designer handbags, and the ability to say "sustainability" while holding a Starbucks cup.

The real kicker? These schools excel at producing Instagram content but struggle to produce athletes who can run without gasping. Football "coaching camps" result in more selfies than goals, and the closest these kids get to global recognition is **tagging Ronaldo in their FIFA game posts.**

Entrance Exams: For Parents Only

Speaking of parents, **Indian school admissions are a different sport altogether.** The kids might get a free pass, but the grilling is intense for parents.

- "Where do you summer?" (Correct answer: Anywhere but your hometown.)

- "What's your child's current reading level?" (Hint: *Peppa Pig* does not count.)

- "Can you afford our fees?" (Unspoken answer: Sell your kidney if you must.)

If you survive this trial, congratulations—you are now the proud sponsor of your child's **unrealistic aspirations** and a school that organises annual days featuring **horse-riding stunts** but no functioning toilets.

The Real Public Schools: Education with a Side of Irony

While the elite schools prance around with **pseudo-global agendas**, the actual public schools sit quietly in the background, doing what they have always done: teaching with minimal resources and maximum resilience.

These schools are where:

- Blackboards double as art canvases.

- Chalk dust is a permanent accessory.

- **Cows wandering into the playground** are considered guest lecturers in "environmental studies."

Lunch is not organic quinoa salad but a **midday meal program** that may or may not arrive, depending on the cook's mood or the state government's priorities. Yet, despite these hurdles, these schools churn out students who know the value of grit and **how to dodge falling ceiling plaster.**

Ironically, these same schools are the breeding grounds for **future IAS officers** and government schoolteachers—who, unsurprisingly, refuse to send their kids to the very schools that built them.

The Contractors of Dreams

Hovering over this comedy are **school contractors**, the unsung villains who ensure every construction project has just enough cracks to require annual "maintenance fees." They boast of "world-class facilities," but looking at the wobbly slides in the playground tells you the world they are referencing is dystopian.

A Two-Tiered Dream Factory

Upstairs, the elite students practice **show-and-tell with Apple Watches**, debating whether their next vacation should be Greece or the Maldives. Downstairs, government school kids create paper boats, dreaming they will float beyond their small worlds someday.

The parents? They are split, too. Elite parents dream of **Stanford** while grumbling about the Wi-Fi speeds in the school's smart classrooms. Government school parents hope their child can pass 10th grade **without selling vegetables after school.**

The Ultimate Punchline

In India, education is not just a system but a spectacle. Public schools are private, international schools are anything but, and parents are left juggling finances and aspirations like **overworked magicians.**

And yet, amidst all the chaos, the **proper lessons** emerge—not from fancy classrooms but from the sheer absurdity of it all, like knowing that dreams are built, not bought and that sometimes, the best education is learning to laugh at the paradoxes of life.

As for me? I will take my memories of chalk-covered hands and newspaper-wrapped lunches over a **"global curriculum"** any day. Because at the end of the day, the real school of life does not charge admission—it just demands you keep learning, laughing, and living.

20

The Great Indian Petrol Pump Chronicles: A Saga of Scam, Stunt, and Smirks

Once upon a time, in the land of *jugaad* (makeshift), a humble traveller stopped at a petrol pump thinking, "Just fuel and go." Little did they know, they were stepping into a meticulously orchestrated carnival of chaos. In this place, frauds flow thicker than engine oil, and your rising blood pressure is the only thing faster than the meter. Welcome to the **Indian petrol pump**, where filling your tank is a test of vigilance, patience, and ability to suppress rage.

The Great Diesel-Petrol Conundrum

Despite giant neon labels, colour-coded nozzles, and stickers the size of a government tender, the first question every filler asks is always the same:

"Diesel ya petrol?"

You glance at your *definitely-not-a-Tractor* vehicle, wondering if you should start wearing a name tag for your bike that says, "Petrol only." But before you can shake your head in disbelief, the second attack comes:

"Premium ya normal?"

You have just rolled in with a wallet already crying, and now they are tempting you with *premium fuel*. What does it do? Does your bike suddenly sprout wings? Will it perform a duet with Arijit Singh? No one knows. You mutter "normal" like a defeated philosopher and hope it is not just rebranded gutter water.

Litres vs. Rupees: A Mathematical Scam

"4 litres, please," you say, innocently thinking this simple request will save you from trouble. Oh, sweet summer child, welcome to **Scam 101**.

Out comes the filler's trusty calculator—older than the petrol pump itself. He inputs some complex equations that would stump even a NASA scientist and declares:

"Sir, ₹420. Arey, ₹500 kar do na—round figure, sir!"

In your confusion, as you mentally calculate how many kilometres ₹500 will get you, the real game begins.

- The meter starts at **₹11.52**, left over from the previous customer.

- The flow rate slows to the pace of a rickshaw climbing a hill.

- And before you can yell, *"Meter dekh raha hoon!"* your tank is magically "full."

If you are lucky, you will notice the **missing half litre** after a week when you are stranded on an empty highway.

The Lightning ₹400 Fill

Even if you channel your inner Sherlock Holmes and ensure the meter starts at zero, the filler deploys his secret weapon: **speed filling**. The meter jumps from ₹0 to ₹400 faster than you can blink, and the nozzle barely touches your tank. You are left wondering if your bike inhaled petrol instead of drinking it.

"Bas bas!" you yell, but the filler smirks. You just got defrauded—and you will realise it only when your fuel gauge gives you the stink eye for the next 50 km.

The Kerosene Cocktail

Ah, adulteration—the petrol pump's pièce de résistance. Everyone knows about it, but no one dares question it. Why? Because the **pump owner is either a local don or his cousin**.

Complaints are pointless. The nearest complaint box is either rusting in a corner or doubling as a plant pot. And suppose you dare to raise your voice. In that case, the filler will summon a **paan-chewing henchman** with " intimidation " as his primary skill on LinkedIn.

The Overfill Scam

"Full tank," you say, not knowing those two words are the fillers' version of a jackpot. The nozzle stays inserted longer than your patience, and before you know it:

- **Fuel spills over.**
- The meter keeps ticking.
- Your wallet gets lighter.

As you stare at the puddle of your hard-earned money soaking the ground, the filler shrugs, "*Sir, overflow ho gaya. Itna toh hota hi hai.*"

The Queue-Jumping Olympics

If you thought the frauds ended at the pump, think again. Enter the **Queue Jumpers**—a species that operates without logic or license plates.

A milkman with a moped older than your grandparents cut the line because "doodh urgent hai." Behind him, a local thug on a spluttering scooter glare at you like *you are* inconveniencing him. The filler? He waves them in because arguing with them is as productive as shouting at a red light.

Receipts: A Mythical Concept

And then, we arrive at **receipts**, the unicorn of the petrol pump experience. Ask for one; the filler looks like you just demanded his firstborn child. The printer is *always* broken, or the roll mysteriously vanished during the last fiscal year. "Sir, kal aa jao," he suggests helpfully as if you have nothing better to do.

The Punchline

By the time you drive off, you have been:

1. **Defrauded on fuel quantity.**

2. **Distracted by fake concern about your tyres.**

3. **Robbed of any remaining dignity.**

And yet, you laugh—because what else can you do? In a land of jugaad and hustlers, the petrol pump is the ultimate stage for **psychological warfare**, and you, dear traveller, are just another willing participant.

So, next time you visit a petrol pump, remember it is not just about fueling up—it is about **staying alert, surviving frauds, and holding onto your sanity**. And, just maybe, pack a spare jerry can. You will thank yourself later.

21

Welcome to Mumbai: The City of Dreams (and Deposits)

Once upon a monsoon in Mumbai—because nothing happens here without rain, even metaphors—a wide-eyed dreamer landed in the city of Bollywood, billionaires, and bafflingly overpriced real estate. Mumbai: where the streets are lined with vada pav stalls, the air is thick with ambition (and humidity), and landowners charge deposits high enough to launch a SpaceX rocket.

The Deposit Dilemma: Paying for Thin Air

The first thing you learn about Mumbai is not its charm but its **"pagri" system**—a sinister term that means *hand over your life savings*. Want to rent a house? Sure, but only if you can fork over 11 months' rent upfront. Yes, eleven months. And no, this does not include the actual rent; that is extra. Why? Because *Mumbai, that is why*.

Picture this: you are staring at a 200 sq. ft. flat in Andheri that costs ₹**35,000 per month**. You are already calculating how many organs you can sell on the black market when the landowner casually says, "Aur ₹4 lakh deposit bhi lagega." Four lakhs? For what? To guarantee that your tears will have a place to pool if your ambition fails.

Chawls: Where Dreams Begin (and End)

When the deposit drama leaves you broke, you find yourself in a **chawl**—Mumbai's iconic slums-cum-survival-training-camps. A chawl room is not measured in square feet but in **how many people it can physically hold without collapsing**. The answer is usually a family of six, two pigeons, a radio older than democracy, and a colony of cockroaches so bold they charge you rent.

Here, privacy is a concept as foreign as snowfall. Your neighbour sneezes, and you say "bless you" without leaving your bed. Conversations between rooms happen through cracks in the walls, and every evening, someone yells, **"Arre light chali gayi!"** (The lights are gone!)

Mumbai Local Trains: The Ultimate Adventure Sport

Of course, life in Mumbai is not complete without the **local train experience**. This daily crucible assesses your endurance, agility, and patience. There is no need to *board* a train here; the crowd *boards you*. You will be swept off your feet, clinging to someone's lunchbox for balance as the aroma of stale fish and sweat becomes your new normal.

And the unwritten rules?

- **Second-class commuters** survive by sheer willpower, hanging out of doors and balancing like circus performers.

- **First-class travellers**, meanwhile, guard their space with glares that could stop traffic. *Accidentally step* *into their compartment.* Congratulations, you are now a social pariah.

Monsoons: Where Potholes Turn to Pools

Ah, the Mumbai monsoon—a season that transforms the city into an Atlantis-themed water park. Roads turn into rivers, auto drivers refuse to go anywhere, and your commute involves a mix of walking, wading, and swearing. Yet, ask a Mumbaikar about it, and they will proudly declare, **"This is the spirit of Mumbai!"**

No, Sunita. The "spirit" is not getting drenched while dodging open sewer holes. It is sheer survival instinct—mixed with an unhealthy reliance on chai and soggy vada pavs.

Vada Pav: The King of Snacks

Speaking of vada pav, let us not forget Mumbai's beloved "burger." It is greasy, spicy, and a surefire way to get acidity by age 25. Still, it is the great equaliser, consumed by everyone from Bollywood actors to office clerks. Rich or poor, there is no escaping its allure—or its aftermath if you are not careful.

Mumbai Dialect: A Symphony of Sarcasm

In Mumbai, language is not just a means of communication but a weapon. The Hindi here is a chaotic blend of Marathi, Bambaiyya slang, and **passive-**

aggressive disdain for outsiders. Terms like "bhaiya" have the same frequency as "timepass."

Marathi sneaks into every conversation, often followed by the classic, **"Marathi shik re!"** (Learn Marathi!) And do not even think about correcting someone's grammar— they will roast you faster than a roadside peanut vendor.

The Rich, the Poor, and the Unreachable Middle

Mumbai is a city of contrasts. You will find billionaires building homes taller than their egos on one side. On the other, construction workers live in the skeletons of those homes, dreaming of the day they can afford a full meal.

Then there is the **middle class**, squeezed between aspiration and anxiety. They spend their lives paying EMIs for a flat the size of a walk-in closet while debating whether to splurge on weekend movie tickets.

The Paparazzi and the People

Mumbai's streets are also home to **paparazzi culture**, where every man with a DSLR is a "celebrity hunter." A stranger feeding a stray dog? *"Mumbai ka naya hero!"* Is someone walking in Marine Drive-in saffron robes? *"Spiritual guru spotted!"*

And do not get us started on the "influencers," who block traffic for Instagram reels while shouting, **"Hashtag Dreamlife!"**

So, Why Stay?

For all its chaos, Mumbai has an undeniable charm. It is a city where you can share a smile with a stranger, sip cutting chai on Marine Drive, and somehow find joy in the madness. Beneath the traffic, frauds, and suffocating crowds, Mumbai is where people dare to dream—sometimes, those dreams come true.

So, welcome to Mumbai. The struggle is confirmed, the spirit is relentless, and the rent is astronomical. But hey, if you survive this city, you can survive anything. And that is worth every sweaty train ride and overpriced deposit.

22

The Great NGO Meeting Saga: A Comedy of Irony and Chaos

Ah, the NGO meeting—a sacred ritual where words are debated, snacks are devoured, and little else is accomplished. Today's agenda? **Opening a library.** Sounds simple, right? Wrong. Even deciding whether to use the word article or item in the proposal can assume a solid half-day in NGOs. Welcome to the labyrinth of jargon, hierarchy, and unintentional hilarity.

The Great Debate: Article vs. Item

The meeting kicks off with enthusiastic energy. A young staff member nervously suggests, **"Should we call the books 'articles' in our library proposal?"** Cue the floodgates of intellectual debate.

"No, 'items' is better!" someone pipes up.

"Article' sounds more professional," counters another, sipping tea like Socrates at a symposium.

"Shouldn't we use the word 'resource' instead?" suggests the Delhi head office representative, prompting audible groans from the field staff.

The room is divided by factions by lunch—Team Article vs. Team Item. The snacks arrive: samosas, biscuits, and chai, consumed with the fervour of starving philosophers, fueling yet another round of debate. No consensus is reached, but hey, at least the chai was good.

The Great Divide: Head Office vs. Field Staff

Then comes the thinly veiled tension between the **head office staff** and the **field workers.** The AC warriors from Delhi sit smugly, their shirts impeccably ironed, while the field team members, smelling faintly of soil and diesel, exchange knowing looks.

Field staff whisper amongst themselves:

"They have no idea what it's like to work in the field."

Head office mutters back:

"If they had better reporting skills, we wouldn't need to micromanage."

The irony? Both sides utterly depend on each other, like two people stuck in a three-legged race, tripping and blaming each other.

The Myth of Convergence and Collaboration

The discussion eventually veers toward *convergence*—a fancy NGO term for **"let's all pretend we're collaborating."** Someone suggests involving the education department in the library project.

"Convergence is key," declares a senior manager, ignoring the snickers in the room. The field team knows the truth: **government convergence** is as accurate as unicorns. At best, you will get a few polite head nods; at worst, you will spend months chasing babus through corridors only to be redirected to the *wrong department*.

Innovation: A Forbidden Word

By now, someone bravely suggests, **"Why don't we try something new for this project?"** The room falls silent. Heads turn. Innovation? What is this sorcery?

A senior member, with decades of *no-risk* strategies under his belt, clears his throat:

"New approaches are risky. Let us stick to tried-and-tested methods."

Translation: "We have been doing it this way since the nineties. We are not fixing it if it ain't broke (and even if it is)." The young staff member sits back down, defeated but wiser.

The Funders: Privileged Sleuths

Enter the funding agency representatives. They stroll in late, exuding an air of privilege. They have never been to a village that does not have room service, but they are here to assess whether the NGO is *"worthy of their generosity."*

With clipped accents and a knack for condescension, they quiz the team:

"How do you measure impact?"

Someone meekly responds, **"We see the children reading books."**

"That is anecdotal. Where are the metrics?" snaps the funder, as if the essence of learning can be crunched into an Excel sheet.

The NGO staff nod and smile, knowing that one wrong answer could mean the project's death sentence. As the meeting drags on, it becomes clear: **the funders do not own the money—they own the power.**

The Gurus of the NGO World

And then, there are the **NGO gurus**—self-proclaimed visionaries who act like they invented social work. They dominate meetings, interrupt everyone, and end every sentence with, **"See, I've been in this sector for 20 years…"**

These gurus love giving sermons about rural life despite having never spent more than an afternoon in a village. During field visits, they stay in five-star hotels and post emotional captions on Instagram about the *"humility of rural India."* Everyone listens to them because no one dares to point out the emperor's new clothes.

Charity and Prestige

Let us face it: working in an NGO comes with zero prestige. Tell someone you work for an NGO at a party and watch their face drop. But if a billionaire donates a fraction of their wealth, it is suddenly front-page news. The irony? You spend your life slogging for change, but the billionaire gets the credit for handing out a few blankets.

The Wrap-Up: Words Over Actions

As the meeting nears its end, there is still no decision on using an *article* or *item*. The snacks are finished, the AC makes everyone drowsy, and the head office staff checks flight schedules. Finally, the chairperson announces:

"We'll form a committee to decide."

Everyone nods, pretending this is progress, while silently wondering if they will ever see this library project come to life. As the meeting dissolves, one field worker mutters to another:

"At this rate, we'll need a library to store all our meeting minutes."

Conclusion: A Symphony of Irony

And so it goes, the world of NGOs—a place where good intentions collide with bureaucracy, where innovation is stifled by tradition, and where even opening a library requires a Ph.D. in patience. Yet, amidst the chaos, people keep trying because sometimes, even the slightest change is worth all the irony in the world.

23

Golgappa, Gupchup, and Pathogens: A Tangy Tale of Culinary Chaos

There is a legend in the bustling heart of Bhubaneswar, where life revolves around traffic jams, temple queues, and the hunt for the perfect street food. **Kalia Bhai**, the golgappa (known as gupchup in Odisha) maestro of Unit 1 Market, is not just a seller—a phenomenon, a magician, and a public health hazard (but who is counting?).

Every morning, Kalia begins his epic journey by waiting for his supply truck, fresh from the land ruled by **Sangeeta Didi**, whose "motherly love" often translates into intense mood swings that could rival a Bollywood plot twist. Thankfully, today is one of her good days, and the truck arrives with Odisha's lifeline: **potatoes.**

Potatoes: The Swiss Army Knife of Odia Cuisine

In Odisha, potatoes are sacred. Forget water, electricity, or Wi-Fi—potatoes are the glue holding society together. They mix with **everything**: meat, fish, pumpkin flowers, even mangoes if you are feeling adventurous (or just deeply confused). Kalia is not after premium spuds; he is hunting for **discount duds**—those half-rotten, oddly-shaped little gems no one else wants. Why? Because in the cutthroat world of gupchup economics, **margins matter.**

The Art of "Hygiene": A Family Affair

Back home, Kalia's **teenage son Hari** takes over. Fresh from an all-night Instagram binge, Hari's hands are sore but determined. He grabs a sack of wheat flour from the local mill, famous for its *"5% invisible discount"* (they just skim some flour off the top).

Hari uses municipal tap water to knead the dough. Now, this is not just any water—it comes with a WHO-approved label that might as well say, *"Drink at your own risk!"* When his hands give out, Hari improvises, deploying a **hand-and-foot kneading technique** that would make a circus performer proud.

Once the dough is ready, **Kalia's wife, Nandi,** steps in. She shapes and fries the puris in **aged palm oil**, which has seen more reheats than your leftover pizza. It is a seven-day-old masterpiece, seasoned with the **essence of history** and a dash of nostalgia (or was that burnt flour?). The puris emerge crispy, golden, and slightly suspicious, ready to meet their fate in the glass basket of Kalia's four-wheel trolley.

The Secret Sauce: Potatoes, Tamarind, and a Pinch of Mystery

Kalia himself takes charge of the **potato mix**, which is boiled to perfection (or until it vaguely resembles mush). Lumps? Extra texture. The **magic happens in tamarind**

water—a potent elixir of chillies, spices, and tamarind pulp, mixed in a pot washed just last week. Is that lingering "aroma"? It is tradition, baby.

Enter the Pathologist: A Tale of Irony and Immunity

Kalia's star customer is **Dr Gupte**, a pathologist who knows more about bacteria than most people know about their families. But science be damned—she has been devouring Kalia's gupchup since childhood, and her gut bacteria now wield swords and shields. Who needs probiotics when your stomach is a medieval fortress?

Dr Gupte does not just eat gupchup; she is its **unofficial ambassador**. She sings its praises to everyone, claiming, *"Kalia Bhai's gupchup doesn't just taste amazing— it builds your immunity for life!"* This kind of endorsement makes WHO officials sob quietly into their clipboards.

The Ultimate Compliment... or Insult?

After polishing off her latest plate of gupchups, Dr Gupte delivers the highest honour Kalia could hope for: *"This is incredible. There is nothing like it."* But then, with the **cheeky smirk of someone who lives for drama**, she adds: *"Of course, though... Katak (Cuttack) gupchup is the best. Bhubaneswar does not even come close."*

Visibly wounded but too professional to respond, Kalia adjusts his basket and prepares for the next customer. His heart might ache, but his gupchups remain unbeaten—at least within Bhubaneswar city limits.

The Gupchup Experience: A Culinary Adventure

Eating gupchup is not just about food—it is an **adrenaline sport**. Will you get tangy tamarind water or taste suspiciously like yesterday's leftovers? Will the puri crack in your hand or explode in your mouth like a water balloon filled with joy? Every bite is a **gamble**, a rollercoaster of flavour, texture, and mild panic.

A Pathogen's Paradise

Health inspectors might argue that gupchup stands are breeding grounds for pathogens, but loyalists know better. *"Germs? Ha! That is just flavour development,"* says one regular. After all, isn't a slight risk the spice of life?

And so, the legend of Kalia Bhai lives on. His gupchups may not win awards for hygiene, but they win hearts—and sometimes stomach battles. If Bhubaneswar thrives, so will its beloved gupchup sellers, armed with potatoes, tamarind water, and enough personality to fill a Bollywood script.

Because in Odisha, gupchup is not just street food—it is a **way of life.**

24

The Auto Chronicles: A South Delhi Drama

On a typically sunny afternoon in South Delhi—where **fashion is life, accents are currency, and attitude is a birthright**—a modern-looking girl stood outside Priya Cinema. She wore **oversized sunglasses so large they could double as satellite dishes** and clutched a venti caramel macchiato like it was the **sceptre of her kingdom**. Her mission? Find an auto to Vasant Kunj.

Enter the Auto-Wala: The Unsung Hero of Chaos

Spotting an auto-rickshaw parked at the corner, she strutted towards it, her designer handbag swinging like a pendulum of privilege. Leaning in with the grace of a Bollywood diva mid-music video, she gave her best pout. In her thick, heavily anglicised accent, she said, *"Bhaaya, will you go to Vasant Kunj?"*

The auto-wala squinted at her, trying to process this alien dialect. Was she speaking English? Hindi? Or some secret language of the privileged? With a puzzled expression, he replied, *"Kya, madam?"* (Translation: "What, madam?")

Unbothered by his confusion, she doubled down, enunciating as if addressing a toddler: *"Bhaaya, Vasant Kunj chalega?"*

The auto-wala scratched his head. Now thoroughly confused, he wondered if she was calling him her **brother (bhaiya)** or casting a **spell**. Gathering his wits, he asked, *"Madam, kya bol rahe ho? Samajh nahi aaya. Dobara bolo."* (Translation: "Madam, what are you saying? I did not understand. Say it again.")

The Breakdown of Communication

With a sigh so dramatic it could have been choreographed, she huffed, *"Bhaaya, Vasant Kunj chaloge or not?"*

At this point, the auto-wala was officially triggered. His **patience evaporated faster than water on a Delhi summer afternoon**, and he fired back with all the sass he could muster:

"Madam, ek toh main aapka bhai nahi hoon, aur doosra, yeh 'Bhaaya' kya hota hai? Bhaiya hota hai, Bhaiya! Aur main nahi jaa raha aapko chhodne!"

(Translation: "Madam, first, I am not your brother, and second, what is this 'Bhaaya'? It is 'Bhaiya'! And no, I am not taking you anywhere!")

With that, he zoomed off, muttering about the **tragedy of modern education** and its inability to teach basic manners.

The Diva's Dilemma

The girl stood there, stunned as if someone had just told her that **avocado toast was now illegal**. She stomped her foot, clutching her caramel macchiato as if it could comfort her. *"How rude!"* she exclaimed, loud enough for the pigeons at Priya Cinema to flutter nervously. *"Like, what even is his problem? So unsanskari!"* (Translation: "So uncultured!")

Her friends—loyal enablers armed with smartphones—had recorded the entire ordeal for their **Instagram stories**. As they muffled their giggles, the girl turned to them and declared dramatically, *"Like, I am **never** retaking an auto. I mean, how can you be so, like, basic?"*

One friend, clearly the philosopher of the group, nodded solemnly and replied, *"Totally, babe. Let us just book an Uber."*

Exit Stage Left: The Search for Trendier Pastures

With a collective air of wounded dignity, the girls sashayed away, leaving the sacred grounds of Priya Cinema in search of a **place where their accents were understood, and their pouts were respected**. For them, Uber was not just a mode of transport—it was a **sanctuary**. In this place, drivers greeted them with five-star enthusiasm, and "Bhaaya" was replaced with "Yes, **ma'am.**"

As they disappeared into the South Delhi sunset, one thing was clear:

The battle for linguistic harmony in the streets of Delhi had been lost, but the war for premium convenience was still on.

25

The Great Indian Train Odyssey: Comedy on Tracks with Extra Masala

First-Class AC: Where Power Meets Pomp

First-Class AC is like a VIP lounge on wheels—but with no free drinks and lots of unsolicited drama. This is where politicians gather to hold loud phone calls that sound like election rallies: *"Vote dena, Bhaiya!"* Meanwhile, their assistants shuffle papers and WhatsApp forwards like it is the **Lok Sabha on tracks**.

Arguments here are not over seats—they are over **coupes**. The VIP squad insists on getting the larger one for their entourage of *"adjusted" relatives*. Meanwhile, a hapless couple in the next coupe sits sandwiched between political fervour and the scent of over-applied aftershave.

Luxury? Yes, if you define luxury as listening to a debate over why the water bottle is not Evian.

Second AC: The "Almost Famous" Club

Second AC is the **middle child of train coaches**—always aspiring to First-Class but forever stuck comparing itself to Three-Tier AC. Passengers here enjoy muttering, *"Bas thoda aur kama liya toh first-class jaayenge,"* while sniffing disapprovingly at anyone who dares use the shared bathroom. Meanwhile, curtain fiddlers pop their heads in every ten minutes, hoping for a scenic view but only catching your frustrated glare.

And oh, the second AC snobs love picking on Three-Tier AC. *"Budget junta hai,"* they whisper, ignoring that their coach smells like damp socks after three stations.

Three-Tier AC: The Chaos Capsule

Three-tier AC is where **dreams, personal space, and footwear hygiene go to die.** It is the melting pot of India, where you are as likely to find a software engineer headed home as you are to encounter a group of college kids playing antakshari like it is the **IPL finals**.

Here, life revolves around one universal enemy: the **middle berth**. Getting into it requires the agility of a gymnast, and sleeping on it involves enough yoga poses to qualify for a wellness retreat. The poor middle-berth soul spends half their journey dodging feet from above and glares from below. The middle-berth warriors in this coach deserve national awards. Bent like human pretzels, they perform the impossible task of existing.

And then come the **unauthorised passengers**, who have mastered the art of *"Bhaiya, thoda adjust kar lo."* Their definition of "adjust" involves occupying half your berth while loudly arguing over their favourite Bhojpuri actor.

Sleeper Class: Jungle Gym of Humanity

Sleeper class is not a train coach but an **Indian version of Survivor**. People sleep everywhere—on the floor, under the seats, and occasionally halfway out the windows. It is the only place to see someone snoring peacefully with one leg dangling into the aisle.

Hammocks appear in luggage racks like **DIY swing sets** and territorial disputes over berths rival international border conflicts. A typical fight sounds like this:

Passenger 1: *"Yeh mera seat hai!"* (it is my seat)

Passenger 2: *"Pehle aap proof dikhao."* (First, you show me the proof)

TTE: *"Arre, dono adjust kar lo."* (Please adjust yourselves)

And food? Sleeper class doubles as a moving street food carnival. Vendors scream, *"Jhal muri! Chai! Samosa!"* At the same time, passengers toss wrappers on the floor like they are auditioning for **India's Got Trash**. The garbage bins exist solely as decor; the real MVP is the aisle floor, which absorbs everything.

Second-Class: The Real-Life Thunderdome

The second class is not a coach; it is a **social experiment**. Here, the luggage racks are hammocks, kids swing like budget Tarzans, and someone sleeps in the toilet. If you thought reservations were respected, think again. The second class operates on one rule: the **loudest voice wins.**

It is also a hotspot for railway freeloaders—people who carry fake IDs and declare, *"Main railway employee hoon,"* as they shove into your seat. You will wonder if they are genuine until you realise their badge is a poorly laminated bus ticket.

Food Fiascos: The Stomach's Rollercoaster

Train food is a crime against humanity, wrapped in foil. Tea is hot water flirted briefly with a tea leaf, and samosas taste like they have survived a nuclear fallout.

But then there are the **Marwari families**—the superheroes of train dining. They unpack entire kitchens from their bags: *poori, achar, laddoo, papad, halwa.* By the fifth station, even the pickiest sleeper-class passenger is drooling. Generous as they are, they offer leftovers to strangers—but only if you pass the *"not too suspicious"* vibe check.

Late-Night Hijinks: The Sleepless Chronicles

By midnight, the train transforms into an **orchestra of chaos**. Snores harmonise with phone calls, and somewhere in the distance, a baby enters hour three of its scream fest. But the true villains? The headphone rebels—or rather, the **no-headphone rebels**.

Armed with loud Bhojpuri music and zero shame, they treat the entire coach to an impromptu concert. Shouts of *"Bhaiya, headphones lagao!"* are met with smug replies: *"Abhi toh party shuru hui hai."*

Toilets: The Horror Show

Train toilets are the **stuff of nightmares**. By the third station, the smell can knock out an elephant. Smokers transform these tiny chambers into cigar lounges, and the bidi smoke mingles with ammonia in an unholy alliance of odours.

The boldest passengers? The ones who clean their bathroom-soaked slippers inside the toilet casually tuck them into bedsheets. Hygiene? That concept left the train two stations ago.

The Great Indian Adjustment Olympics

If Indian trains had a motto, it would be: **"Thoda adjust kar lo."** From sharing berths with strangers to letting families take over entire compartments for birthday parties, the art of adjustment is sacred.

Somehow, amidst the chaos, there's beauty. Passengers share snacks, argue like family, and form friendships that outlast the train journey. Because at the end of the day, **Indian trains are more than transport—they are cultural carnivals on wheels.**

Life on Tracks: A Symphony of Absurdity

Indian trains are the beating heart of the nation. They are chaotic, loud, hilarious, and uniquely human. Whether you are squished into a corner of sleeper class or arguing over a coupe in First AC, every journey is an adventure.

And when you step off the train, curry crumbs on your lap and Bhojpuri beats still ringing in your ears, you know one thing for sure: **you have just lived the most authentic slice of India.** Bon voyage!